TRAPPED!

"I'm going to the barn to meet our friend," Nick said. He took two steps out the door and then there was a shot.

Stephanie shouted and Nick leaped back through the door into the safety of the house. He moved cautiously back to the door and peered out.

"Are you going to shoot back?" Stephanie asked.

"With this?" Nick replied, indicating her little .25.

"Does that mean we're stuck? Like sitting ducks?"

"No. I'm going to make a run for the car."

"Nick!"

"I'm not going to leave," he said hurriedly. "I'll drive the car into the barn. Maybe I can flush him out—or get close enough to face him with this peashooter of yours."

NICK CARTER IS IT!

"Nick Carter out-Bonds James Bond."
—*Buffalo Evening News*

"Nick Carter is America's #1 espionage agent."
—*Variety*

"Nick Carter is razor-sharp suspense."
—*King Features*

"Nick Carter is extraordinarily big."
—*Bestsellers*

"Nick Carter has attracted an army of addicted readers . . . the books are fast, have plenty of action and just the right degree of sex . . . Nick Carter is the American James Bond, suave, sophisticated, a killer with both the ladies and the enemy."
—*The New York Times*

FROM THE NICK CARTER KILLMASTER SERIES

THE DEATH DEALER
DEATHLIGHT
THE DEATH STAR AFFAIR
THE DECOY HIT
THE DOMINICAN AFFAIR
THE DUBROVNIK MASSACRE
THE GOLDEN BULL
THE GREEK SUMMIT
HIDE AND GO DIE
THE HUMAN TIME BOMB
THE HUNTER
THE INCA DEATH SQUAD
THE ISRAELI CONNECTION
ISTANBUL DECISION
THE KALI DEATH CULT
THE LAST SAMURAI
NORWEGIAN TYPHOON
OPERATION VENDETTA
THE OUTBACK GHOSTS
THE PARISIAN AFFAIR
PLEASURE ISLAND
THE REDOLMO AFFAIR
REICH FOUR
RETREAT FOR DEATH
THE SATAN TRAP
SIGN OF THE COBRA
THE SNAKE FLAG CONSPIRACY
SOLAR MENACE
THE STRONTIUM CODE
THE SUICIDE SEAT
TIME CLOCK OF DEATH
THE TREASON GAME
TRIPLE CROSS
TURKISH BLOODBATH
WAR FROM THE CLOUDS
THE YUKON TARGET

NICK CARTER

KILLMASTER

THE DECOY HIT

CHARTER BOOKS, NEW YORK

Dedicated to the men of the Secret Services of the United States of America

THE DECOY HIT

A Charter Book/published by arrangement with The Condé Nast Publications, Inc.

PRINTING HISTORY
Charter Original/October 1983

ISBN: 0-441-14221-4

Charter Books are published by The Berkley Publishing Group, 200 Madison Avenue, New York, New York 10016.
PRINTED IN THE UNITED STATES OF AMERICA

PROLOGUE

Howard Clark had been an agent for enough years to know when he was being tailed. On a night when most people would be huddling in their homes to escape the wet and the damp of a misty London fog, why else would the same figure be behind him, a block away, for the past twenty minutes?

Clutching the courier pouch which was beneath his raincoat, close to his body, Clark began to take some evasive action. If the man was good, he wouldn't be able to lose him, and that would verify his belief that the man was a tail. If that were the case, he would have to take steps to "cut off his tail."

It was early evening and, despite the dreary weather, many shops and stores were still open. He picked several stores for their size, which would indicate that they should have more than one entrance and exit.

He entered each store, trying to blend in with the other shoppers while working his way toward an alternate exit.

Four times he did this, and four times he discovered that the man was still there.

So, he *was* a tail, and he *was* a professional.

It was time to take stronger action. Lead the man somewhere quiet, where he could take care of him with a minimum of attention.

Clark knew London well, and he knew just where he

wanted to take his tail so that he could perform the "amputation."

It was an alley in a part of London which had once been prosperous, but had fallen on hard times. Where there had once been many little out-of-the-way shops, and some residences, there were now only boarded-up buildings and empty streets.

And an alley that suited Clark's purpose. The mouth of the alley was small, but it opened into a nice-sized cul-de-sac. As he crossed the street toward it, it would have been plain to anyone watching that he was heading for that particular alleyway.

"Alleyway" was a generous way to describe it, because as he walked through, his shoulders almost simultaneously rubbed both walls.

He came out into the cul-de-sac and moved to the side, flattening his back against the wall. The man would be foolish to follow, but rather than lose Clark, he would have to.

Clark stood quietly, controlling his breathing, listening for the footsteps of his tail. In his right hand he held his gun, a Browning that he had used for years. His left arm was flattened against his side, with the pouch nestled between.

Clark had also been an agent long enough to realize when he had made a mistake.

Listening intently for any sounds coming from the alleyway, he heard instead a sound from *behind* him. Before he could react, someone grabbed him by his wet hair, pulling his head back so that the entire length of his neck was exposed.

As he felt the sharp blade slice across his throat, splitting the skin and severing the arteries, he knew in a flash that he had made a mistake, that he had spotted the back tail, and had totally missed the front tail. He had been "double-tailed," and failing to notice that fact had been a fatal mistake. . . .

ONE

People in the espionage field—men and women—know that they are involved in a very serious business; still, many of them often refer to it as "the game."

"That's the way 'the game' is played."

"You've got to play by the rules of 'the game.' "

"Somebody has to win, somebody has to lose. It's just like 'a game.' "

It's a game, and they are "the players."

David Hawk, the head of the super secret government agency called AXE, seemed intent on making it more of a game, however. That's the way it seemed to Nick Carter, anyway. When Nick arrived at his boss' office in the Amalgamated Press and Wire Services Building on Dupont Circle in D.C., he was invited to have a seat, and then he was asked an odd question.

"When you were a child, N3, did you ever have a peg board?"

"Excuse me, sir?" Nick asked, not sure he had heard Hawk correctly. In all the years Nick had known and worked with the older man, they had never discussed the subject before.

"A peg board," Hawk said again. "You know, one with different-sized holes, all different shapes, and you have to fit the proper-sized peg into the proper hole?"

"Uh, I believe I did, sir, yes," Nick replied, still puzzled.

"Don't frown at me as if you think I've gone senile, N3," Hawk said sharply.

"I'm sorry, sir," Nick said hastily, "I didn't realize—"

"Never mind," Hawk said. He opened his top drawer and took out a metal cylinder that looked like it probably contained a very expensive cigar.

"This is for you," the older man said, extending it across the desk to Nick.

"I don't much like cigars," Nick said, accepting it from him. Hawk ignored the remark.

"You have in your hand the object of what we call 'Project Round Peg,' " Hawk explained.

Nick turned it over in his hands and said, "Looks like a round peg, all right."

"It is, practically speaking," Hawk replied, "and your job is to find the round hole that it will fit into."

Nick shook the cylinder and asked, "What's in it?"

"Knowing that is not important to your assignment."

"Am I playing in the dark again, sir?" Nick asked. "That was one thing I didn't like to do as a child."

Nick shook the cylinder again, but for all the reaction he got from inside, it could just as well have been empty. It *felt* light enough to be empty.

"If you've finished with your remarks, I'll get on with my explanation," Hawk said dryly.

"Oh, yes, sir, go on, please," Nick said, closing his hand around the object and resting his hands in his lap.

"You knew Howard Clark, I believe?"

"Yes, sir, I know—uh, sir? Knew Howard, did you say?"

"Yes. His body was discovered in London yesterday. He'd been missing for several days." Hawk paused, then added, "His throat had been cut."

Howard Clark had been a colleague of Nick's until he jumped agencies, going to the DIA years ago. He was one of the Defense Intelligence Agency's best men—and now he was dead.

"Does his death have anything to do with this?" Nick asked, holding up the "round peg."

"Yes," Hawk answered, "it does. Clark was acting as a courier at the time of his death."

"Carrying this?"

"No. He was carrying something that was vital to the DIA, but the point is that he was the fourth United States courier killed this year. It has to stop, Nick."

"I agree, wholeheartedly," Nick Carter said. "Do we know who has been knocking off these couriers?"

"No, we don't."

"Not even whether or not it was one particular country, or an independent operator looking for something to peddle?"

"We don't know," Hawk said. "I've met with the officials of other intelligence agencies, and even putting our heads together, we can't figure that part out."

"And there's nothing coming down the pipeline?"

"No."

"How vital is the information that we've been losing?"

"It is vital, but not critical," Hawk replied. "If another country has already purchased it, we wouldn't necessarily hear about it."

"And what about this?" Nick asked, holding up the cylinder.

"That," Hawk said, pointing with the index finger of his right hand, "is vital, which is why you've been chosen to deliver it."

"Dcliver it where?"

"Not where, but to whom."

"All right, to whom?"

"This man," Hawk said. He passed Nick a five-by-seven photo of a gray-haired man in his early sixties. "Dr. Anton Lector."

"And where is he?"

"Well, up until yesterday he was in London."

"Up until yesterday," Nick repeated. "The same day Clark's body was found?"

"Yes."

"Connection?"

"Only in that the incident seems to have spooked him into going underground."

"I think I'm getting the picture now," Nick said, everything finally adding up. "I'm supposed to deliver this little doodad to Dr. Lector, but first I've got to find him."

"Correct."

"At the same time, I've got to be on the lookout for whoever has been knocking off our couriers."

"Correct, again."

"So this is the 'round peg,' and Dr. Lector is the 'round hole,' " Nick summarized.

"Exactly."

"I assume you've got me booked on a flight to London."

"Tonight," Hawk said, nodding. Again his hand dipped into his top drawer, and he said, "Here's your ticket," handing an envelope to Nick. He took it and tucked it away in his inside breast pocket.

"In that envelope you will also find the last known address of Dr. Lector while he was in London."

"Well, then, that's the place to start," Nick said, standing up. "You realize that he not only may have gone underground, he may have left London altogether."

"I realize that, yes," Hawk replied. "Talk to our people in London, N3. If you decide that the doctor has gone to some other country, you will just have to go after him."

"Luckily, my passport is in order."

Hawk stood up and said, "I don't have to tell you to be careful, or to stay in touch."

"No, sir, you don't."

"Very well. You are the man we decided was most able to carry the round peg, N3. Please don't let anything happen to it."

"Don't worry, sir," Nick told him, holding the object in front of him. "I'll treat it as if it were the best of Cuban cigars."

TWO

When Nick Carter left David Hawk's office, there was someone waiting for him in the outer office.

"She said she was waiting for you, Mr. Carter," Hawk's secretary informed him.

"Is that so?"

He looked at the young lady in question and found her to be quite easy on the eyes. She was about twenty-four, with auburn hair that did not quite reach her shoulders. She had very clear brown eyes and a very smooth, pale complexion. Her body appeared to be full and firm. She was very pretty, indeed. Under normal circumstances, he might have been trying to think of an approach to use on her, but these were not normal circumstances.

Nick wanted to know how she knew where to find him, and what she knew—if anything—about the Amalgamated Press and Wire Services Building.

"*Are* you waiting for me?" he asked her, approaching the chair she was seated in.

She stood up immediately, revealing herself to be better than five feet seven.

"Are you Nick Carter?" she asked.

"I am."

"Then I'm waiting for you. I would like to talk to you about Howard Clark—if you have some time."

Nick frowned and asked, "What do you know about Howard Clark?"

"All that there is to know," she answered. "I'm his daughter."

Daughter, Nick thought. He knew that Howard had a daughter, but he thought she was . . .

She smiled and interrupted his thoughts by saying, "You thought I was a little girl."

"Yes."

"So did he," she said. "Can we go somewhere and talk?"

"Uh, sure, I've got a little time," he said, wondering if she knew that her father was dead. "Let's go downstairs and have lunch somewhere."

"That's fine."

During the years that Nick had known Howard, he had always talked about his "little girl," but this wasn't a little girl anymore. She had grown up, and filled out.

He was trying to remember her name—or remember if he'd ever even known it—while they picked out a place for lunch. They finally settled on a small steakhouse cleverly called "The First Family."

When they were seated and had placed their orders, she leaned her arms on the table and said, "My father talked about you quite a lot. I thought you would be older."

"I am," he assured her.

She smiled and said, "He liked you."

"I liked him, too," Nick answered before he realized that they were both speaking in the past tense. In that moment, her name came to him and he said, "Stephanie, you know—"

"Yes, I know my father's dead," she said, interrupting him. Her mother had died, he remembered, during the time that Howard had worked for AXE.

"I'm sorry."

"I know you are. You were one of the few men my father liked in this business."

"You know about your father's business?"

"Oh, yes," she said, rummaging about in her handbag now. "I told you I knew all there was to know." She found what she was looking for and added, "This might make you feel a bit easier about talking to me."

She withdrew her hand from her handbag and handed him a laminated photo identification card identifying her as an employee of the Defense Intelligence Agency. Unlike AXE, the DIA was not a covert agency. Nick examined the card and handed it back to her, convinced that it was the real thing.

"You see?" she said. "We're in the same business."

"What is it you do for the DIA, Stephanie?" Nick asked.

She replaced the card in her handbag—probably in the exact same spot, because it took her just as long to put it back as it had for her to get it out. After she had it safely tucked away, she looked at him with a sheepish expression on her face and said, "I, uh, I'm a file clerk."

"Okay," he said.

The waitress came with a salad for her and a medium steak for Nick, and they suspended conversation while she set the plates down.

When the waitress left, Stephanie Clark said, "All right, so I'm only a file clerk. I still want to know what happened to my father."

"Stephanie, you know what kind of business your father was in," Nick reminded her.

"Sure, I know," the girl answered, "but that doesn't mean I just have to accept his death. I want to know how, and why."

"Why have you come to me? Haven't you taken it up with the DIA?"

"The DIA also thinks of me as just a file clerk," she said.

"My father was the best man they had, Nick, but he always said that you were the best there was in the business."

Nick didn't quite know what to say to that, so he remained silent and cut into his steak.

"Nick, I want you to find out who killed him."

Nick started to shake his head and she exclaimed, "Why not? You were his friend."

"A lot of my friends are dead, Stephanie," he informed her. "I don't have the time to go out and find out who killed them all. It's part of the game."

"Damn you!" she hissed, but not so loud that anyone else in the place could hear her. "That's just what they've been telling me at the DIA, that it's a game and dying is part of it. Well, I don't buy it!"

"I'm sorry, Stephanie," Nick said. "I couldn't look into your father's death if I wanted to. I've been given an assignment—"

"You're the great Nick Carter, aren't you?" she demanded, standing up. "You could if you wanted to, but you just don't want to. I guess my father was wrong about you. From where I stand, you don't look so great."

"I'm sorry you feel that way. . . ."

"I'll find out myself," she went on. "That's what I'll do. I'll find out who killed him by myself."

Nick grabbed hold of her wrist before she could walk away and said, "This isn't a game, Stephanie."

"Well, that's what everyone's been telling me it is, including you."

"Don't act like a child."

She yanked her wrist from his grasp and said, "What have you got to do that's so important that you can't find out who killed your friend?"

She turned without waiting for an answer and stalked out of the restaurant, which was just as well.

What would she have thought if he had told her that he had to go find a round hole for a round peg?

As Nick Carter left his office, David Hawk sat back in his chair and marveled at how his job often precluded him from being honest with his men—most notably, Nick Carter.

How many times, he wondered, had he sent agent N3 off on an assignment without even telling him half of the truth? As a Killmaster, Nick Carter was a professional who followed his orders to the letter, and never veered from his assigned course—unless, of course, it suited his purpose, the successful conclusion of his mission.

Hawk recognized that it was N3's individuality that made him the finest of AXE's operatives, which was why he had been entrusted with this particular assignment—armed this time with input that was far less than half the truth.

There was, however, the one indisputable truth that existed almost every time Hawk sent N3 out to play his part in the game—that it could result in the death of Nick Carter.

THREE

Nick stared out his hotel window and wondered why it rained almost every time he came to London. He had seen much of what this great city had to offer from beneath the eaves of an umbrella.

Nick had arrived in London just an hour earlier. Upon entering his room at the London Hilton, he immediately placed a telephone call to a prearranged number, the response to which he was now awaiting with impatience. Problems at each end of his flight had caused him to arrive much later than anticipated, and he was anxious to get started on his assignment.

While waiting for the call, he had called room service and ordered a pot of coffee and a bottle of bourbon. One was gone and the other half gone, and the call still had not come.

He filled in the time thinking about Howard Clark and his "little girl," Stephanie. He hoped the girl wouldn't try anything foolish, but if she was anything like her father, then she was not short of courage and determination; yet she was just young enough to temper those with impetuosity. The three made a dangerous, volatile combination.

He had just decided to have no more bourbon and ordered a second pot of coffee, when the phone rang.

"Mr. Carter?" a man's voice asked. It sounded young, but that was an excuse for stupidity.

"You must have the wrong room," Nick said coldly.

"Oh, yes," the voice said, half to himself, and then, "I thought this was room N3. Did you, uh, did you want an estimate?"

"Christ, yes," Nick said, "and it's about time."

"I'm sorry I couldn't call sooner," the man replied, "but when you were delayed, I became delayed. . . ."

"All right, let's forget all the delays," Nick suggested. "What have you got for me?"

"Nothing."

"You've heard nothing at all?" Nick asked. "That means that at least he hasn't turned up in the hands of some foreign government."

"Not so you'd notice," the man said. He was obviously American, as there was no trace whatsoever of a British accent.

"All right, who checked the house?"

"One of our people."

"I'll check it again."

"We've checked—"

"So I'll check it again. If I need anything, I'll call you."

"As you wish," the man said, sounding insulted. "Good night."

"Yeah, good night."

Nick hung up and silently began cursing airplanes and airports. If he'd arrived earlier, he could have checked out the house tonight. Now he'd have to wait until morning.

Or would he?

Dammit, why should he?

He threw on his coat, checked his personal arsenal—Wilhelmina, Hugo, and Pierre—and then left the room. It was only ten P.M., which, when you thought about it, wasn't that late at all. And he certainly wasn't ready to retire for the evening, so he might as well go to work.

He left the hotel without an umbrella, turned up his collar, and asked the doorman to get him a cab. True, an umbrella would have made sense in the rain—if he were a banker. It also occupied one or both of his hands, and he needed them free at all times. He'd much rather be alive and wet than dead and dry.

He gave the cabbie the last known address for Dr. Lector and sat back to think about his job. The "round peg" was tucked away in his inside breast pocket. He could have hidden it in his room somewhere, but a pro would have found it no matter where he put it. It was better to have it on him and know where it was at all times. To take it away from him, someone would have to kill him and then it wouldn't much matter to him anymore where it was.

Nick was not normally assigned courier work, but with the way United States couriers had been dropping, this was a little more than just routine courier stuff. Nick had three jobs. One, find Lector and deliver the round peg; two, stay alive; and three, stop whoever has been killing the American couriers.

Not necessarily in that order, of course.

When the cab stopped, Nick paid the driver and got out, hunching his shoulders against the rain. He scanned the rows of doorways for the right number and then climbed the stairs. Stepping into the foyer, he found six mailboxes. Naturally, the name Lector was not on any of them. There was, however, an A. Lester, which showed a great deal of imagination on somebody's part. The flat was on the second floor, so Nick rang the two third-floor doorbells and was admitted by an obliging tenant. He hurried to the second floor and moved into the shadows while someone on the third-floor landing came out and peered down the steps.

"Cheeky kids," a man's voice said in disgust, then Nick heard the retreating footsteps and a closing door.

He moved down the hall to A. Lester's room and, using lock picks, let himself in. Once inside, he drew all of the curtains and turned on a small lamp. Going into the kitchen, he searched for and found a dish towel, then took it back into the living room with him and set it on the floor against the door so the light wouldn't show in the hall.

That done, he removed his wet coat, draped it over a chair, and then studied the layout. Living room, bedroom, and kitchen. Three rooms, and a comfortable enough looking place.

Checking the bedroom first, he found drawers half filled with clothes and a closet to match.

"The doctor left in a big hurry," he said to himself. Aside from the clothing, there wasn't much else to be found, so he checked the kitchen next. He didn't know what he was looking for, so he didn't skip anything. He checked cereal boxes, sugar bowls, anywhere a man could conceivably hide something, but came up empty each time. Moving to the living room, he fared no better. The doctor had left in a hurry and hadn't left anything behind to indicate where he might have gone.

Nick shrugged back into his coat, which hadn't had time to dry, and glanced around one last time. If there was anything there to be found, he would have found it. This was a dead end, and once he left, there'd be no reason for him to come back.

Now he could either go back to his hotel and get some sleep, or he could walk out the front door and try and put himself into Anton Lector's frightened shoes.

Where would I go if I was a frightened scientist afraid of getting killed if I stayed in one place for too long?

The only problem with putting himself in the man's shoes was that the man was not a pro. His movements would be made not from logic, but from emotion.

Nick left the apartment, pulling the door shut behind him, locking it automatically. He checked the stairwell, found it empty, and made his way to the ground level. He was in the foyer, with his hand on the outside door, when something tugged at his eyes. It was just a flash of white, but it was enough to make him turn his head and look at the row of mailboxes.

There was an envelope, or a sheet of paper, in the mailbox marked A. Lester. Nick removed his hand from the doorknob and went over to the boxes. Using Hugo, his trusty knife, he pried the top of the mailbox off and reached inside. It was an envelope addressed to "Dr." A. Lester, and the return address was Paris, France.

He tucked the envelope into his inside breast pocket and left the building.

FOUR

When Nick stepped outside, he found that the rain had tapered off to a light drizzle, but it was still chilly enough for him to turn up his collar.

As he started down the stairway to the street, a chill ran down his spine, and it had nothing to do with the weather. He hadn't heard the shot, but the sound of the bullet glancing off the iron railing was very audible, and he moved instinctively.

He vaulted the railing to his right, and as he fell to the ground, he found that the drop was much deeper than he had anticipated. The dark had hidden the fact that there was a stairwell leading down. It was like stepping off a roof into space without knowing how high the roof was. His stomach lurched as he continued to fall, trying to keep his feet under him, and then halfway down he struck the stairway with both feet. As he landed, one foot slid out from under him on the wet stairs, and he lurched forward head first down the remainder of the steps. He struck a concrete wall with his shoulder and bounced off, falling to his hands and knees in a puddle a couple of inches deep.

Although he was dizzy from the fall—both falls—and the rough landing, his unique instinct for survival was still working. Whoever had fired the shot was probably on his way across the street to check on his success or failure. Nick had moved so quickly that the would-be killer might have thought that the impact of the shot had knocked him over the railing.

Nick looked up the steps and realized that if the killer came upon him now, he had nowhere to run. The man could just stand at the head of the steps and fire a shot down. Even if he missed, it would ricochet off the concrete walls enough times to finally find its mark.

Still on his knees, Nick reached out with his right hand and encountered wood, not concrete. He staggered to his feet and fronted the door, finding it locked.

"Shit," he said. He tested it and although it was flimsy, he felt it might hold against his shoulder. He produced Hugo again and began to force the blade of the sharp knife between the door and the doorjamb. With a satisfying click, the bolt clicked back and the door opened inward. As he stumbled into the darkness, a shot rang out. As he shut the door behind him, he heard the sound of the slug ricocheting around, and then striking the door.

There was no time to catch his breath. The shooter would be on his way down the steps now, and the door wouldn't stop him any longer than it had stopped Nick. Of course, N3 could have stood and fought, waiting with his gun out for the man to come busting through the door, but on the off chance that he came out second best, he didn't want the "round peg" he was carrying to fall into the wrong hands.

He felt for a light switch, found one, and turned it on. A weak twenty-five watt bulb bathed him in dim light, but it was bright enough for him to find a two-by-four on the floor. He picked it up, jammed one end against the wall opposite the door and the other end against the door. It was an almost perfect fit. He stomped on the lower end in order to wedge it in more, and then started down the hallway toward a flight of stairs.

As he ascended the stairs, he could hear the would-be assassin pounding on the door. Even if the man fired through the door, smashing the lock, the two-by-four would still hold.

When Nick got to the top of the stairs, he encountered a closed door and hoped it would not be locked. He was in luck. As he turned the knob, the door opened and he stepped into another hallway. He accidentally slammed the door behind him, and a few moments later, a door in the hallway opened and a woman stepped out, spotlighted by the light coming from her room.

"Who's there?" she called out.

"Don't be alarmed, miss," Nick called out.

"I ain't alarmed, ducks," she said, "but you look to be. What are you doing out here?"

Nick found himself breathing hard, and his shoulder and knees were starting to ache. The shoulder was the result of slamming it into the wall, and the knees no doubt had taken the brunt of his landing.

"Would you believe," he said, "that I'm trying to avoid an irate husband?"

The woman appeared to be in her early thirties—although the dimness of the hallway might have been kind to her—and well-built. She was wearing a robe that was open, revealing a scanty nightie that barely covered her heavy breasts.

She peered at him to get a better look, then straightened and posed with her hands on her hips.

"Seeing how pretty you are, luv," she said, "I'd say that was very bloody likely. Would you, uh, like to hide in here?" she asked, flicking her finger in the direction of her room.

"That sounds like a good idea," he said.

"Step in, then, luv," she said, moving aside to allow him room. She didn't give him too much room, though, and he had to brush against her breasts in order to enter. She followed him closely and shut the door behind them.

"How many other rooms on this floor?" he asked.

"A few rooms and some other doors as well, ducky," she said. "Your irate husband wouldn't want to wake everyone up by pounding on all the doors, would he?"

He hoped not. The man—or woman, now that he had time to consider—would have to make a split-second decision. If he stopped to bang on doors, he might be giving his quarry time to get further away—and that was if and when he got by that two-by-four. He might have given up on the door and gone back up the steps, waiting for Nick to come out of the building by some other door.

"Can I get you a drink?" she asked him. "You look like you could use one."

"Thank you."

Inside the well-lit apartment, Nick found that she looked to be in her late thirties, with long black hair, dark eyebrows, full, ripe lips, and just the hint of a second chin developing.

"Do you mind if I sit?" he asked.

"Not at all, luv," she answered. "I'll get you that drink."

He took his coat off first, draped it inside out on a chair to avoid getting anything wet, then sat down and took stock of the damage.

Both knees of his pants were wet, but not ripped, and his knees were aching something fierce. Likewise, his left shoulder, which had struck the wall. He was lucky that he hadn't struck his head. If he had, he'd have been a sitting duck.

The apartment was very warm, and he found the source of heat coming from a portable heater that was plugged in and set against the wall opposite him.

"Whiskey all right?" she asked, coming into the room carrying two half-filled water tumblers.

"Just right," he said, taking one.

"It's neat," she added, sitting next to him. "You don't look like the sort of man who would ruin good whiskey."

"I'm not," he said, and tasting the drink found that it was indeed good whiskey.

"Your pants are wet," she said, putting a hand on his knee. "Take them off."

"What?"

"I said take them off, luv. I'll hang them on the back of a chair by the heater. They'll be dry in no time."

"That's all right—"

"Come on, luv," she said, putting her glass aside and going down on one knee. "Get them off. We'll have to start with the shoes first. Ooh, they're sopping wet, as well."

She undid the laces on his shoes and took them off, then felt his socks and took them off as well.

"Now the pants," she said, grabbing for his belt.

The tip of her head was just under his nose, and she smelled clean and fresh, as if she had just stepped from a shower or bath. The situation was ludicrous. Here he was with a strange woman who was undressing him, and there might be a killer in the hall looking for him—although he doubted that. Chances were good that the man was either gone or waiting outside somewhere. He didn't want to take a chance on leaving too soon. Just in case the latter was true.

But in spite of the ridiculousness of the situation, he found himself responding physically to the nearness of the woman.

"What's your name?" he asked as she tugged his pants off. "I think we've come to a point in our relationship where I should know that."

"My name's Cordelia Grey," she said, taking his pants and hanging them on a chair by the heater. "There, they'll dry quickly there." She turned to face him and said, "I'm a secretary, living here because it's all I can afford." She looked around, then said, "It looks terrible, doesn't it? About all I can do is keep it clean."

And it was that, Nick thought, as the warmth from the heater seeped into his muscles.

"Look at those knees!" she exclaimed.

"What about them?"

"Well, aside from being pretty," she said, "they're bruised up pretty bad."

He took a closer look and found that she was right. He must have struck them on the ground after he bounced off the wall.

"Guess they do look sort of messed up," he said, grimacing as the ache in his shoulder flared.

"What else is wrong?" she asked, looking concerned.

"Banged my shoulder up," he said, "falling down those outside steps."

"You fell down the steps?" she said. "That fella must have been pretty big for you to be in that much of a hurry to avoid him. You look like you're in fine shape."

"I was," he said, grimacing again.

"Maybe I can help you," she said. "Take off your shirt."

"My shirt?"

"A hot compress and a massage might be just what your shoulder needs, before it gets much worse."

"You've already done enough, Cordelia," he protested, but she wasn't having any of it.

"Just drink your drink and I'll be right back." She started out of the room, then turned and said, "You haven't told me your name. Aren't we at that point in our relationship yet?"

He smiled at her and said, "My name is Nick."

"Sit tight, Nick, luv," she said, "and I'll be right back."

While she was gone, Nick struggled to his feet and tried to walk to the door, but found that his knees had stiffened up on him. Forcing the issue, he shuffled to the door and pressed his ear against it, but there was nothing to be heard. He had just lowered himself back on the couch when Cordelia came back with a hot compress.

"You still have your shirt on."

"Cordelia, you've been very kind—"

"Don't argue," she said firmly, and began to unbutton his shirt. He caught the hint of a new scent and realized that she must have put on perfume.

"Cordelia, could I have a little more of that bourbon?" he asked.

"Will you take off your shirt while I get it?"

"Yes."

She nodded and took his glass with her.

Nick hurriedly shrugged out of his jacket and shoulder holster and wrapped Wilhelmina in the jacket so that she wouldn't show. He pushed Hugo into the package as well, along with Pierre. It wouldn't do for Cordelia to see his personal arsenal. It might frighten her into screaming—although he doubted she was the screaming type. She seemed to be a very competent woman, and not as flighty as she might have first appeared. The apartment was clean, and so was she, and he felt that she didn't belong in an apartment this beneath her.

"Here you are," she said, coming back in, "and you've got your shirt off. Good." He noticed that she had secured the front of her robe.

She handed him the glass and then walked around behind the couch. The T-shirt he was wearing was a tank-top style, making it easy for her to put the compress right on his shoulder.

"This looks pretty badly bruised, as well," she said, touching the muscle with her fingers.

She alternated between massaging the muscle and holding the compress to it, until it was no longer warm.

"That's enough of that," she said, putting it aside. "Just let me work on it a little more." She touched his shoulder again. Nick wondered if she could notice the erection that was straining at the front of his shorts.

He heard a whisper of cloth, and then, as she massaged his shoulder, he suddenly felt something on the back of his neck. Hard points rubbed the skin on his nape, and he suddenly realized that what he felt were the swollen tips of her breasts.

"This is crazy," she breathed suddenly. She pressed her chin down on the top of his head and rested her heavy breasts on his shoulders so that the back of his neck was nestled in the warm valley between them. Her hands traveled down, and she ran them over his hard chest muscles, rubbing her palms over his nipples. "Crazy," she said again, "but this whole situation has me more excited than I've been in years, Nick, right from the moment I saw you in the hall." She reached down further with one hand, sliding it beneath the waistband of his shorts, and she added, "You too, I see."

"Yes," he said, catching her wrist. "Me, too. Come around here where I can reach you."

She removed her breasts from the back of his neck and joined him on the couch, naked. Her breasts were large, and the nipples and aureola were a dark brown, with darker brown freckles on them in places.

He placed the palm of his hand over one of them, and she closed her eyes and leaned into his touch. He bowed his head and caught a nipple gently between his teeth, first rolling it about, and then sucking on it.

"Let me," she said, sliding from the couch and crouching between his legs. "Let me . . ."

He leaned back on the couch and closed his eyes, feeling the heat—the heat of the portable heater, the heat of the bourbon, and the heat of her mouth as she drew on him. . . .

"Is there a back way out of here?" he asked her later.

"Don't—" she started to say, but stopped. They were lying in her bed, having moved there from the couch a couple of hours before. She pressed her head against his chest and said, "There are a couple, but one way leads to an alley that goes into the next street, Marigold Lane."

"I have to go," he said.

She kissed his chest, licked a nipple until it was hard, and then rubbed her cheek against it, saying, "I know, I know."

As he dressed, she said, "This was wonderful, Nick, but—"

"But what?" he asked.

"We won't ever see each other again, will we?"

He hesitated, then saw no point in lying.

"I doubt it, Cordelia."

"You weren't running from an irate husband, were you?" she asked, then held her hands up and said, "No, you don't have to answer that. Forget I asked."

She slid from the bed and started to get dressed, saying, "I'll show you that door."

He nodded, then went to the living room for the rest of his clothes. By the time she came out, he was dressed, with all his weapons back in place.

"This way," she said, opening the door.

"Wait," he said, rushing to her and pulling her away from the doorway. He checked out the hallway first, making sure it was empty, then said, "All right."

She gave him a strange look, as if she were realizing what strangers they really were, then walked past him and led him down the hall. At the end they had to turn either left or right, and she took him to the right and showed him the door to the alley.

"This is it," she said.

"Cordelia—" he started, but she pressed her fingers to his lips, then kissed him hard, but fleetingly. "Good luck, whoever and whatever you are . . . and thank you."

She hurried back down the hall, and he watched until she

was out of sight. Quite a woman, he thought. She deserved more than a night with a stranger, no matter how wonderful it had been between them.

He was sorry he couldn't give her more of himself, but he had already given her more than he should have.

FIVE

Nick had a few anxious moments when he stepped out into the alley. He hadn't realized that it would be that narrow. It was hardly more than a space between two buildings, and he would have to turn sideways to negotiate it. While he was in that small space, he'd make an easy target from either end, but it had been hours since the attempt on his life, and he chose to believe that a second attempt had been put off until another time.

When he came out into Marigold Lane, it was still dark, and the rain had stopped completely. With about an hour before the sun would start to come up, he headed back to his hotel where he could soak in a hot tub and catch a few hours sleep before he renewed his search for Anton Lector.

His clothing had dried well, and as he walked through the lobby of his hotel, he drew no curious glances. He walked directly to the elevator, rode to his floor, used his key, and entered the entrance foyer of his room. There was a closet and a small couch there, and further on was the actual bedroom.

As he hung up his coat, he suddenly became aware, by virtue of instinct only, that he was not alone in the room. He withdrew Wilhelmina from her holster and reached for the light switch, which was not in the room itself, but in the foyer. He flicked it on, and as bright light bathed the room, he rushed in and fell to one knee, holding his Luger out in front of him.

"Jesus Christ!" Stephanie Clark snapped. "You scared the wits out of me."

She was lying fully dressed on his bed, which was still made, and had obviously been asleep.

"Stephanie," he said, breathing a sigh of relief that he hadn't killed her. "What the hell are you doing here?"

"I told you I was going to do some investigating on my own," she reminded him, straightening her skirt so that it covered her knees. "I followed you here," she said.

"You followed me?" he asked, incredulously. Surely she hadn't been able to follow him without his seeing her. Was he slipping that badly?

"Well, not followed you in the true sense of the word," she said. "I found out that you were coming to England, so I came, too."

"How did you find out?"

"DIA contacts," she said. "Top secret."

"The DIA knew I was coming here?" he asked, rising to his feet. He didn't like that, and what's more, he didn't understand it.

"I tapped into their main computer from the terminal in my office," she explained. She noticed the look on his face and said, "Don't look so grim. The DIA knows a lot of things about a lot of people."

"Not about me," he said. "How did you get in here?"

"I took a room of my own, then asked for yours—"

"I'm not registered under my real name," he said, interrupting her. He was liking this less and less.

"I described you to the clerk, gave him a sad story and a tickle under the chin, and then let myself in."

"Something else you learned from a DIA computer, I suppose?" he asked, taking off his jacket and shoulder holster.

"Not exactly," she said, smiling coyly. "I went out with

one of their agents for a while, and he taught me a thing or two."

"I'd love to know his name."

"So you could report him?" she said. "No way."

"What do you want, Stephanie?" he asked, peeling off his shirt. His shoulder was stiff and he needed a good soak in a hot tub.

"I just wanted to let you know I was here," she said, swinging her feet off the bed and onto the floor.

"Now that I know, would you mind going back to your own room?" he said. "I've got to take a bath."

"Sure you don't want me to stick around and scrub your back?" she asked.

"Don't get cute with me, I'm not in the mood," he warned.

"I can see that," she said. "What kept you out so late?" she asked, approaching him. Suddenly, as she was almost up to him, she seemed to stiffen and take a step back. Seeing the look on her face, Nick knew that she had gotten close enough to smell the telltale signs of another woman on him. The odors of a woman's perfume, and a man and a woman's passion.

"I see what kept you," she said. She moved to her left and picked up her bag from the bed. "I'll leave you alone, since it's obvious that you need your rest from a hard night's work."

She marched past him to the door, then turned to hit him with a parting remark.

"I wonder what my father would say if he knew that instead of looking for his killer, you were—"

"I told you in Washington, Stephanie, that finding your father's killer is not my job."

"That's right, you did," she said, "but I told you that it is my job, and I'm going to do it."

"Just stay out of the way while I do mine!" he shot back.

"I wouldn't want to be anywhere near you when you do what you do," she sneered, and left, slamming the door behind her.

Just what he needed, he thought as he filled the tub with hot water, an amateur—and a girl besides—"mucking about," as they said in this country, getting in the way and trying to get herself killed.

Finding her father's killer was not his job, but it also was not his job to stand around and watch her get herself killed.

Damn it.

SIX

Nick soaked in the tub for a good half hour, giving the hot water time to sink its warmth into the muscles of his knees and shoulder. Wilhelmina was within easy reach on the counter next to the tub, just in case. If Stephanie had been able to find him, why not his would-be assassin? In the morning he was going to have to move to another hotel, and also get in touch with the AXE agent here in England. Then he would contact Hawk, concerning the DIA knowing his whereabouts and allowing a file clerk access to their computers.

While he was drying off, he thought briefly of Cordelia Grey, then pushed her out of his mind. There was no room there for a woman he had only known a few hours, no matter how intimate the circumstances had been.

He put on a robe, picked up Wilhelmina, and walked out of the bathroom. His eyes fell on his jacket, hanging over the back of a chair, and he remembered the envelope he had taken out of the mailbox and tucked into his pocket.

He put the gun in his robe pocket, picked up the jacket, and removed the envelope. Whoever had addressed it to "A. Lester" had made the mistake of writing "Dr." before it, probably out of habit.

He took the letter and sat on the bed with it. The return address had no name on it, but it did have a Paris address.

Opening the envelope and taking the letter out, his fears were confirmed when he saw that it had been written in French.

The only thing that he was able to read clearly was the name in the salutation. It was "Anton."

SEVEN

Nick slept with his Luger underneath his pillow, and when he woke up, he made two phone calls, one to room service for breakfast, and the other to the coded number. He was almost finished with his continental breakfast by the time the call was returned.

"Room N3?" the voice asked. It was the same voice he had spoken with the night before.

"You got it right this time," Nick said. "Congratulations."

"Well," the man said, "did you find anything that *our* people missed when you went to—"

"Yes," Nick said, before the address could be mentioned, "I did."

"You . . . did?" the man asked, sounding disappointed and puzzled.

"I need someone who can read French," Nick said, and then as an afterthought added, "and speak English. You got that?"

"I've got it."

"Today."

"I'll do my best."

"Just do it right and I'll be happy. Call me back in an hour."

"I can't—"

"In an hour," Nick said again. "After that I won't be here anymore."

"I'll do my best," the voice said.

"Shit," Nick said, and hung up.

Fifty minutes later, the phone rang while he was packing.

"All right," the voice said. "Where?"

"In the lobby."

"The lobby? Why not your room?"

"I don't have a room here anymore," Nick said. Right after he had hung up earlier, he had called the desk and told them to make up his bill. "So it's the lobby. I'll be sitting there with a brown two-suiter. Got it?"

"I've got it. Half an hour."

Nick hung up, picked up his bag, and left the room, pulling the door shut behind him. He just hoped he wouldn't run into Stephanie during the next half hour.

Nick sat in the lobby for forty minutes, keeping one eye on the front door for his interpreter, and the other on the elevators for Stephanie. He passed the time by trying to guess who the interpreter was. At one point, a classy-looking brunette walked in and he found himself hoping it was her, but she walked to the front desk, spoke to the clerk, and left again.

After forty minutes, a nondescript man of average height and average weight entered, looked around, spotted Nick's brown two-suiter, and then started for him. Now this, Nick thought, looks like an interpreter.

"Are you the owner of this two-suiter?" the man asked in perfect English.

"Yes," Nick said, standing up. "Come on."

"Where?" the man asked, looking puzzled.

"You'll see when we get there." Nick picked up his suitcase and repeated, "Come on."

They went outside and Nick asked the doorman to get them a cab. When they were in a cab, Nick told the driver, "Just drive around for a while."

"Whatever you say, Guv," the man answered. With the meter running, he didn't care if he had to drive around all day long.

"What is the meaning of this?" the interpreter asked.

"Shouldn't matter to you where you do your job, as long as you get it done," Nick said. He reached into his pocket and took out the letter. "I want you to tell me what this says," he instructed the man, handing him the single page.

"This is very irregular," the man complained. "I'm not used to working under these sort of conditions."

Nick didn't like the way things had been going right from the beginning. First his contact sounded like a beginner, then Stephanie shows up and tells him that the DIA is keeping tabs on him. Now this prima donna didn't like having to read on the run. To top it all off, his knees and shoulder still ached.

"Look, I'm sorry I couldn't set you up in the best hotel in town just to read this thing, but I don't have time for that. Tell me what it says or I'll let you off—without stopping."

"You wouldn't dare!"

"Sounds to me like he would, friend," the cabbie said.

"Thanks," Nick said. He looked at the other man and said, "Well?"

"Very well, as you wish," the man said. He started to read the letter aloud: "Dear Anton, Received the time and date of your arrival. Have told no one, as you instructed. Hope you will tell me what is wrong when you arrive. I look forward to seeing you, old friend."

"Very concise," Nick said.

"What does it mean?" the man asked, handing it back to Nick.

"That's not part of your job, pal," Nick said. He tucked the letter away again, leaned forward, and tapped the cabbie on the shoulder. "Let my friend out anywhere along here."

"You can't do that!" the interpreter said.

"I'm sure you can find your way back," Nick said.

The cab pulled over and Nick reached past the man to open the door.

"Thanks for your help."

The man rushed from the car, as if in a hurry to put as much distance between himself and Nick as possible.

"Okay, let's go," Nick told the cabbie.

"Where to, Guv-nor?"

"Paris."

"You're joking."

"Then make it the airport, and I'll take it from there."

EIGHT

Outside of Orly Airport, Nick took the fourth in a line of cabs and told the driver to drive around for a while.

"As you wish, m'sieur," the man said, assuming that he simply had another crazy American as a passenger.

When he was sure that he hadn't been followed from the airport, Nick gave the man the name of a small hotel he knew of off the beaten path; he had stayed there before.

"A good choice, m'sieur," the driver said. "I know of this place. The food is *magnifique*."

Which was not exactly the reason Nick was going to stay there, but it certainly didn't hurt.

At the hotel, Nick paid the cabbie and tipped him generously, then went in and approached the desk.

The clerk, who was also the assistant manager, looked up from his work to greet the new guest, and then his face lit up as he recognized Nick.

"M'sieur Stuart," the man expounded. Whenever Nick stayed there, he used the same name, Nick Stuart. This was sort of a safe house for Nick, in that his "business" had never intruded on his stays there.

"Hello, Henri."

"And how long will you be staying this time?" the assistant manager asked.

"I'm not sure, Henri," Nick said, registering.

"As if you ever do, eh?"

Nick grinned, took his key, and carried his own bag up to his room on the second floor. He didn't know what the assistant manager thought his business was, but the man rarely failed to fulfill a request of his, and did so without question.

Before going up, he asked, "Could you have a pot of coffee brought to my room, please?"

"Of course," the man replied happily. "Would you like anything with it?"

"Some pastries, perhaps," he answered.

"Very well. You shall have them shortly."

"Thank you, Henri."

"It is our pleasure to serve you, Mr. Stuart," the assistant manager replied with a curt bow.

Nick went upstairs and was about to unpack, but decided not to. There was no telling when he'd have to leave or how short notice there would be.

The coffee and pastry were delivered by Henri himself, who once more told Nick what a pleasure it was to have him as a guest once again. When he left, Nick found both the coffee and the cake delicious, as he had remembered, but reminded himself that he was not in Paris to reacquaint himself with past pleasures.

He took the letter to "Dr. Lester" out of his pocket, checked the address again, then tucked it away and left the room. Out front, he flagged down a passing cab and gave him the address. Ten minutes later, he was in front of the building, paying the driver.

He checked the number on the building against the number on the envelope, then mounted the front steps. It appeared to be a two-story private residence, with one bell and a single mailbox out front. He pushed in the bell button and waited for an answer.

He didn't know exactly what he expected, but it wasn't

what he got, that was for sure. The door was answered by a dark-haired, almond-eyed beauty who looked him up and down and asked him what he wanted, in French.

In English he replied, "I'm looking for a Pierre LaMouche. Does he live here?"

"You are American," she said, making it more of a statement than a question.

"Yes."

"Is there something I can do for you?" she asked. "I am Marie LaMouche."

"Well, Mrs. LaMouche—" Nick began.

"Miss," the girl said, cutting him off. "Pierre LaMouche is my father."

"I see. I'm sorry," Nick said. "Is he in?"

"He is not," she answered, "and that is why I have asked you if there is anything I can do."

"I'm afraid not," Nick said. "I really wanted to talk with your father."

"In that case . . ." she said, starting to close the door.

"Uh, excuse me," he said, putting his hand out to stop the door. She looked first at his hand, and then at his face.

"Yes?"

"When will he be back?"

"Perhaps this evening."

"Perhaps?" he asked, hoping she would elaborate.

"Oui, perhaps. Good-bye, m'sieur."

"Good—" he said, but the door had already been closed. "—bye."

An extraordinarily lovely girl, he thought, but very rude. In fact, almost too rude. She hadn't even asked him for his name.

Could that have been because she already knew who he was? Had she been waiting for him to ring the bell just so she could tell him that her father wasn't home—even if he was?

Nick descended the front steps, but he already knew that he'd be coming back later—and next time he wouldn't ring the bell first.

NINE

When Nick entered the lobby of his hotel, he saw Henri break out into a wide smile.

"M'sieur," Henri greeted. "Have you had a nice morning?"

"I've had better, Henri," Nick said. "Is everything all right?" he asked, frowning at the hotel man.

Henri's eyebrows did a dance over his eyes, and he said, "Oh, oui, m'sieur. Everything is just as you like it."

"I wish," Nick said. He walked toward the stairs to the second floor, looked back at Henri, who was still grinning from ear to ear, and then went up, frowning.

When Nick got to the door of his room, his sixth sense was working overtime. Henri's behavior had set it off, and he realized that someone was in his room. He didn't draw his gun, but he kept his guard up as he slipped the key into the lock and opened the door.

"I don't believe it," he said.

"Believe it," Stephanie Clark said from her seat on his bed.

He closed the door behind him and threw his key down on a table.

"Stephanie, what are you doing here?"

"Just keeping up with you."

Yeah, he thought, but how? Something was wrong here.

She was an amateur and she was with him every step of the way.

"The DIA computer again?" he asked.

"Trade secret," she said.

He took off his jacket and loosened his tie before telling her, "This isn't doing you any good, you know. You may be following me, but I'm not looking for your father's killer."

"That's all right," she said. "He'll find you."

"If he doesn't find you first." He pulled a chair over so that he could sit near her without sitting next to her on the bed. "Stephanie, go home before you get hurt."

"You think I'm just an amateur, right?"

"Right."

She grinned at him and said, "I haven't done too badly so far, have I?"

No, she hadn't, at that. And she couldn't have used the DIA computer in Washington this time, either.

"If you want me to leave, I will," she said, "but I'll be around Nick. . . ."

"I didn't say I wanted you to leave," he assured her.

"You don't?"

"No. Maybe you're right. Maybe we will accomplish more working together."

"Do you mean it?" she asked excitedly.

"Yes, I mean it," he told her. He didn't tell her that he wanted her to stay so he could keep an eye on her. "I'll call downstairs and see if we can get you a room."

"Can't I stay here?" she asked.

"No, you can't," he said. He dialed the desk and spoke to Henri, asking him if there was a room available.

"I am sorry, M'sieur Stuart, but there are no rooms available this evening."

"And in the morning?"

"I am sure I will have one in the morning, m'sieur," he replied.

"All right," he said. "Reserve one for my . . . guest, will you?"

"Of course, m'sieur," Henri said, "and have a very pleasant night."

He could see in his mind's eye Henri's grin, and he said, "Thank you, Henri."

"I will send the young lady's baggage up to your room."

Nick hesitated, threw a glance at Stephanie, and then said, "You do that."

He hung up and turned to Stephanie.

"How did you get the clerk to let you in?"

"It wasn't all that difficult," she said. "I intimated that we were . . . friends, and he didn't seem surprised. He agreed very willingly to let me in to wait for you."

Nick seemed to remember having Henri allow a lady into his room once or twice before, and he wasn't surprised that the "romantic" assistant manager had given in to Stephanie so easily. She was, after all, a very lovely young lady.

And this was France.

TEN

"You look like a burglar," she said later, after he had changed his clothes. He was now wearing a dark turtleneck sweater and dark pants, and over it, he put a dark, nylon windbreaker. "If you had white socks on, you'd really look funny."

"I'll bet," he said. He took out Wilhelmina, checked her, and then slid her back into his holster. He watched Stephanie and saw that the gun made her nervous.

"You don't like guns?"

"Is that part of the deal?" she asked. "I have to like guns?"

"No, you don't have to like guns," he told her, "but it might be good for you if you knew how to use one."

"I'll leave that to you," she said. "So, are you going to tell me?"

"Tell you what?"

"Where you're going?"

"Out."

"We're not married, you know," she said.

"What's that mean?"

"That's the kind of answer a husband gives a wife when he's going to see another woman."

"Is that so?" he asked. "Is that from personal experience?"

"Don't avoid the issue," she said. "Are you?"

"Am I what?"

"Going to see another woman?"

"Are we married?"

"No."

"Then I don't have to tell you, do I?" he said, heading for the door. "I'll be back soon. Keep the door locked."

"Bring back something to eat," she called after him. He was going to tell her to call room service, but then he'd just told her to keep the door locked.

"Okay."

"Bring french fries!" she called as he went out the door.

As he walked through the small lobby, he saw Henri grinning at him and waved back. Outside, he flagged a cab and had it take him to the home of Pierre LaMouche.

"Right here," he said when they were a block away.

"Zis eez not—" the driver started in terrible English, but Nick waved him off.

"This is good enough," he said, paying him and getting out. He waited for the cab to drive away, then made his way to the LaMouche house on foot.

He had no doubt that every time he went to the house and rang the bell looking for Pierre LaMouche, his daughter, Marie, would tell him that her father wasn't at home. That meant that he had to get into the house and to LaMouche without ringing the bell.

Nick circled around to the back of the house and used his lock picks on the back door. He found himself in a dark hallway, and up ahead bright light was coming from a room.

Moving quietly, he worked his way down the hall toward the lighted doorway.

He could hear voices coming from the room, but couldn't make out what they were saying. They were talking too low and too quickly in French.

Since he had no desire to frighten anyone, when he reached the doorway, he made some noise so that the occupants of the room would hear him. That was less frightening, he thought, then his simply appearing.

As it was, Marie LaMouche turned to face him with a gasp, while the other person in the room merely stared wide-eyed at his sudden appearance.

The other person was an elderly man.

"Pierre LaMouche?" he asked, addressing himself to the man.

"*Sacre bleu*!" the girl exclaimed when she recognized him. "It is *you*."

"It's me," he agreed.

"Papa, this is the man I told you about, who came to the door asking for you."

The old man nodded to her, then looked at Nick and asked, "Have you come to rob us?"

"You know why I'm here, Mr. LaMouche," Nick said. "I think you both know, which is why your daughter lied to me today."

"I did not—"

"Marie," her father said in a tired voice. She looked at the old man and then lapsed into silence.

"Tell me what you want?" the man asked Nick.

"Anton Lector."

"I do not know the name."

"You know the name," Nick said, "and the man as well."

"I tell you I do not—" the man started to repeat, and as he did, Nick reached into his pocket and approached him. The old man flinched and his daughter gasped, as if they expected Nick to produce a gun, but Nick dropped a folded envelope into his lap and then stepped back.

"What is this?"

"It's a letter that you mailed to Dr. Lector. Apparently he left England before the letter arrived. I found it in his mailbox and it led me here."

LaMouche unfolded the letter just enough to verify its authenticity, then put it aside.

"Who are you?"

"I'm someone who has a delivery to make," Nick said. "I'm supposed to give something to Dr. Lector, but he got frightened and ran. I can't stop until I find him and give him what I have."

"A bullet?" Marie asked sarcastically.

"No, not a bullet," he said.

"Then what?"

"Marie," her father said again, more forcefully.

"I can't say what," Nick said to LaMouche. "M'sieur LaMouche, you know what kind of work Dr. Lector does."

"No, I do not," the old man said. "It is secret, that much I do know."

"Then believe me when I tell you that what I have for him is vital to his work. I must give it to him."

"If it is so vital, why is he running from you?" Marie LaMouche asked.

Nick looked at her father, who merely shrugged his shoulders as if to indicate that he had tried.

"Miss LaMouche, it's not me he's running from, I can assure you of that."

"Who then?"

Nick decided to take the time to elaborate, if it would keep her quiet. Without her, he might have had the old man convinced already.

"I have two assignments, Miss LaMouche," he said. "One, to find Dr. Lector, and two, to kill a man." He saw her eyes blaze briefly when he said that. "The man he is running from is the man I must kill, but I cannot do that until I find the doctor and make my delivery." He turned to her father and said, "Please, I need your help. Is he here?"

The old man looked at his daughter, who shook her head, but he made his own decision.

"No, he is not here."

"But he did come here."

"Father—"

"Marie, please!" her father snapped. To Nick he said, "Yes, he did come here, but he left two days ago."

"Why?"

"He was afraid that he had stayed too long," LaMouche said.

"He thought someone was hanging around the house," Marie said. "He was very nervous."

"*Was* someone hanging around the house?"

"We did not see anyone," LaMouche said. "Anton is my friend, but just because he thought he saw someone does not mean that someone was there."

"I understand," Nick said. Lector might have been so scared, he was seeing bogymen under the bed.

"Did he say where he was going from here?" he asked.

"Papa!" Marie said sharply. "You trust too easily."

LaMouche looked at his daughter, and then back at Nick.

"Perhaps my daughter is right," LaMouche said, "but, nevertheless, I have told you all I know."

"You don't know where he went?"

"I do not. Anton felt safer not telling me."

"May I see the room in which he was staying?"

"Of course," the old man said. "My daughter will show it to you."

"Thank you, M'sieur," Nick said.

"Follow me," Marie LaMouche said and, stiffbacked, walked from the room as if she didn't care whether he followed her or not.

He followed her up a flight of carpeted steps to the second floor, where she took him to a small, modestly furnished bedroom.

"The guest room," she said, opening the door and stepping aside.

"Did he unpack while he was here?" he asked.

"I did not check his drawers," she said.

He made one round of the room, opening drawers and closet doors, but nothing was left—if anything had been in them at all.

"Find anything?" she asked.

"Not yet," he said. He stood in the center of the room, looking around for something he might have missed.

And then he spotted it.

He walked to the writing desk across the room and bent over to inspect the trash bucket.

"What do you expect to find in there?" she asked.

"Not much," he said, sticking his hand in, "but I'll take what I can get."

There was a five-by-seven writing pad on the desk top, and in the garbage was a number of crumpled pieces of paper. He took the pieces from the bucket and stuffed them into his pockets, and then he picked up the pad from the desk.

"May I take this?" he asked.

"If you need paper that badly."

He took the pad and walked over to her.

"Why are you so hostile?" he asked her.

"Since you ask, I will tell you," she said. "I am hostile toward anyone who endangers my father's life. I did not want Dr. Lector here, and I do not want you here."

"That's fair enough," he said. "I'm leaving."

They went back downstairs where Pierre LaMouche was sitting just where they had left him. Nick wouldn't have been surprised if the old man had not even blinked an eye.

"Thank you, M'sieur LaMouche," he said.

"You find Anton safely, m'sieur," the man said.

"I'll do my best."

Marie LaMouche walked to her father's side and put her hands on his shoulders protectively.

Not one to get careless, no matter what the situation, Nick backed out of the room and down the hall and let himself out the back door.

Two blocks from the house, Nick flagged a cab and gave him the address of the hotel. They hadn't gone a mile when he remembered that Stephanie had asked for something to eat. French fries, she had said. Where the hell was he supposed to find french fries in Paris?

And then he saw something he couldn't believe: golden arches.

"Right there," he said to the cab driver, tapping him on the shoulder and then pointing.

When the cab pulled up in front of the place, Nick stared at it for a while, then said, "I'll be damned," and went in and got Stephanie what she wanted.

When he walked into the lobby carrying the bag with the food in it, it was the first time he had ever seen Henri without that smile—or some kind of a smile—on his face.

"M'sieur!" Henri said in horror.

"It's not for me, Henri," he assured the man. "It's for my guest. You know how American women are."

"Oui," Henri said, giving Nick a world-weary look.

"Why don't you just send your specialty up to my room for me while I bring her this."

"Oui," he said again. "As you wish."

When he unlocked the door to his room and entered, Stephanie was sitting cross-legged on the bed wearing a terry-cloth robe.

"You're going to get me kicked out of this hotel," he said to her accusingly.

"Why?"

He held up the bag for her to see and she bounded off the bed shouting, "McDonald's!"

ELEVEN

Henri brought Nick his food about twenty minutes later and cast a weary glance at Stephanie as she was finishing off her third bag of french fries.

"What's eating him?" she asked Nick when the man had left.

"It's not what's eating him," Nick said, inspecting his own food, "it's what you're eating."

"He doesn't like french fries?"

"I don't know a Frenchman who does."

"What are you eating?"

Nick sat down at the tray bearing his dinner, and said, "Blanquette de veau."

"What's that in English?" she asked.

"Delicious," he answered.

She came over and looked at it, and then said, "It looks like veal."

"That's what it is," he said. "Veal stew."

"Can I taste it?"

"Pull up a chair," he invited. There was a second plate on the table, and he put a small portion on it and gave it to her.

She put a small piece into her mouth and said, "Oh, it's delicious!"

"I'll tell Henri you said that," Nick said. "It just might redeem us."

As if to leave little or no doubt of her sincerity, Stephanie went on to eat half of Nick's dinner and drink half of the bottle of wine that Henri had included.

"That was yummy," she said, smiling dreamily.

"Are you drunk?" he asked her.

"Heavens, no," she said. "It takes more than a half a bottle of wine to make me drunk." Then she added, "I am little snookered, though."

"I thought so. I think you better go to bed."

"Ooh, Mr. Carter, is that an invitation?"

"It's a suggestion, Miss Clark, and nothing more."

"Pooh," she said, pouting.

"Off with you."

She got up and walked to the bed, and after turning it down, she asked, "Where are you going to sleep?"

"I'll put a couple of chairs together or something," he said. "Don't worry about me."

"Oh, but I do," she said, removing her robe to reveal a flannel nightgown that extended to her ankles. "I'm putting you out of your bed."

Her nipples were poking little hills in the front of her nightgown as she got into bed.

"You've been putting me out ever since I met you, Stephanie," he said. "Why should it bother you now?"

"Don't be mean," she said, pouting again.

"I wouldn't dream of it," he assured her. He got up and wheeled the tray out into the hall, leaving it there to be picked up. When he turned around and shut the door, he heard Stephanie's even breathing and knew she had fallen asleep.

Convinced that she wasn't shamming, he went to her purse and started looking through it. He didn't know what he was looking for, but he was hoping to find something that would explain her to him. He found the usual items one finds in a woman's handbag, plus her DIA identification, her ticket and baggage stubs for her flights to England and

France . . . and a gun, a little .25 caliber automatic, fully loaded and in need of a cleaning.

He put everything but the gun back, then pulled out the pad and paper he had taken from the LaMouche home.

First he unraveled the papers he'd gotten from the trash can and smoothed them out as best he could. It appeared that Anton Lector was one of those people who liked to doodle while he was thinking.

Each piece of paper had random words and drawings on them. Nick was sure that a psychiatrist would probably be able to tell a lot from them, but he wasn't a shrink and they didn't mean anything to him at all, except maybe to indicate how frightened the doctor was of being killed. Twice he had drawn stick figures of men, with one killing the other.

Nick put the discarded pieces of paper aside and turned his attention to the pad. Actually, all he was interested in was the top sheet. He held it up to the light to see if there were any impressions on it, but the imprints that were there were all jumbled. Apparently, Lector was heavy-handed, and the impressions left were from more than one page. Tracing over them with a lead pencil wouldn't tell him a thing.

Tossing the pad down, he figured that it had been too much to ask for anyway.

He sat down and began to clean Stephanie's .25 for her. Not that he expected her to use it, but if she did, it would be better if it didn't explode in her hand.

TWELVE

In the morning, Nick woke with a stiff back from the two chairs he'd slept on. He called down and had breakfast sent up to the room, but didn't wake Stephanie until it arrived.

"Up and at 'em, Mary Sunshine," he said, slapping her on her blanketed behind.

"What?" she yelled, snapping her head up and looking around wide-eyed.

"Hey, take it easy," Nick said.

She looked around for a few more seconds, obviously disoriented, and then looked at him and seemed to recognize him.

"Oh, Nick," she said. She pushed herself up and twisted into a seated position beneath the blankets. "I forgot where I was for a few moments."

"How do you feel?"

"Okay," she said, "aside from a little headache."

"That's from half a bottle of wine."

"Did I really drink half a bottle of wine?" she asked.

"Enough to put you to sleep."

"I must have been tired for it to affect me that much."

"Enough for you to invite me into bed with you."

"I did that?"

"You did," he said. "Breakfast is here. You want to eat and then clean up, or—"

"I'll eat," she said, bounding off the bed. Her gown was bunched up around her waist, and he was treated to the sight of her pale, flashing thighs as she rushed to the breakfast tray.

"Did you order enough?" she asked.

"I hope so," he said, eyeing her dubiously.

He had ordered two continental breakfasts, but she ended up eating half of his, as well.

"So what did you do after I, uh, went to sleep?"

"I did some reading," he said truthfully.

"Anything interesting?"

"I don't know for sure," he said. "I couldn't really make heads or tails of it."

"I've read books like that, too." She stood up and said, "I'm going to take a shower. What's on our agenda for today?"

"Getting you your own room is first," he said. "After that, I'm afraid I'm lost."

She frowned and said, "I can't tell if you're kidding or what."

"Don't worry about it," he advised her, "just go and take your shower."

While she was in the shower, he disposed of the breakfast tray by putting it in the hall, then sat down again with the pieces of paper he had taken from the LaMouche house. They still didn't tell him anything and he left them atop the small writing desk next to the door.

When Stephanie came out with one towel around her head and another covering her vital parts, she said, "It's all yours."

Seeing the steam that was trailing out of the room behind her, he said, "Maybe I should wait until the smoke clears."

She looked behind her, then laughed and said, "I like to take hot showers."

"I'll bet," he said. What flesh he could see was all rosy and glowing from the hot water, and he couldn't help but wonder about the parts he couldn't see. "When I come out, I'll check with Henri about your room."

"Why?" she said. "I don't mind sharing yours, and you've been a perfect gentleman."

"Yeah, well, you can't count on that indefinitely," he said, and closed the bathroom door behind him.

When Nick came out of the bathroom with a towel wrapped around his waist, Stephanie was waiting for him—in bed.

"What's this?" he asked. "Going back to bed?"

"Not just me," she said, "and this time I haven't drunk half a bottle of wine."

"Stephanie—"

"Come on, Nick," she said. "I'm only trying to save us the cost of an extra room. I mean, if we're working together, we're sharing the cost, right?"

"Right," he said warily.

"Then come here," she said. The blanket was rolled down to the foot of the bed, but she still had the sheet over her, molding itself tightly to her full breasts so that the nipples were clearly outlined. He felt himself rising beneath the towel as he approached the bed.

She touched the front of the towel as he grasped the sheet and threw it back.

Her normally pale skin still had a rosy hue from the temperature of her shower, but her nipples were standing up as if they had been splashed with cold water. He palmed one and then the other as she freed the towel and allowed it to fall to his ankles.

"Come on, Nick," she said, grasping him firmly in her hand. "I'm not a virgin and I'm not going to break."

She didn't break, either. She was firm and strong as she

clasped him to her with her arms and thighs, and she raked his back while he drove into her. When they both achieved a simultaneous orgasm, she squeezed him to her even tighter, milking him dry, and then she relaxed beneath him and said, "See, I told you I wouldn't break."

He kissed her and her mouth opened wide beneath his.

"I never thought you would, Stephanie," he said, moving off of her to lie beside her. "Is there something else I can call you other than Stephanie?"

"Don't you like my name?"

"It's fine. It's just a little long, especially for moments like this."

"I don't have another name," she told him, "unless you want to call me Steffie. I haven't been called that since I was a kid."

"I guess I'll stick with Stephanie," he said.

"Make up your own nickname for me," she proposed, snuggling up close to him.

"I'll think about it," he said, getting out of bed.

"Where are you going?"

"To see about your room."

"But I thought—"

"Sorry, kid," he said, picking up the phone. "I'd love to have you around, but it would be too dangerous for you."

She frowned and was about to say something else when he spoke into the phone.

"Henri, it's Mr. Stuart."

"Ah, m'sieur. How did you enjoy your, eh, evening?"

"It was fine, Henri."

"Dinner, and—"

"Dinner *and* breakfast were excellent, as always."

"Ah, merci, m'sieur!"

"Henri, do you have that room ready for my friend yet?"

"It is being cleaned even as we speak, m'sieur."

"You'll need her name for your register," Nick said.

"It's Williams, K. Williams."

"Kay?" Henri asked. "That is her first name?"

"That's her initial," Nick said. "Her name is Kit, K-I-T, Williams."

"A strange name," Henri said. "Very American, no?"

"Very American, yes," Nick agreed. "Call my room when it's ready, Henri."

"As you wish, m'sieur."

"Kit?" Stephanie asked him as he hung up.

"Kid, Kit, it's all the same. Just a name to use."

"And a name for you to call me," she said. She pulled on her robe and said, "I'm going into the bathroom to get dressed. Let me know when the room is ready, will you?"

"Sure."

He watched her as she walked into the bathroom and shut the door behind her.

She'd been good in bed, maybe too good. And her attitude had changed, too, from the time he'd picked up the phone to the time he'd hung up.

It was a troublesome thought, but maybe she wasn't really the amateur she made herself out to be.

Maybe she wasn't even *who* she made herself out to be; but if that was the case, then who was she?

"Your room is ready," he told her when she came out of the bathroom, looking fresh, well-groomed, and lovely.

"Thanks for the use of yours," she replied, and then with a pointed look, added, "and your bed."

"Anytime."

"Sure," she said, gathering up her things.

"It's right down the hall," he said. "I don't know how Henri worked that out, but he did."

"He's a Frenchman," she said, as if that explained it away.

Nick was fiddling with the pieces of paper on the writing

desk, and she said, "I was looking at those before."

"Really?"

"When you were in the shower. What do they mean?"

"That's what I'm trying to figure out," he said. "What did they mean to you?"

"Not much," she said, "except to remind me of how much I enjoy skiing in Switzerland."

"Why Switzerland?" he asked.

"This picture here," she said, turning over another sheet. "This chalet is one of the most famous in Switzerland—if you're a skier. I recognize it because I've skied there before."

"I see," Nick said.

"Would you like to help me to my room?" she asked, breaking into his thoughts.

"Huh? Oh, sure, I'll carry your bag, lady," he said, making himself sound like a bellboy. "You better be ready to tip well, though."

"I already tipped you," she reminded him, looking at the bed. "Or did you forget?"

"No," he said, "I couldn't forget that."

"Why are you holding on to that particular drawing?" she asked, as he began to stuff it in his pocket.

"This is the one that's going to tell us where to go next," he said.

"Switzerland?"

"You'll find out," he said, picking up her bag. "Come on, let's get you settled in your room."

They walked down the hall to a room where the door had been left ajar.

"The key should be on the table next to the bed," he said as they entered.

"It's here," she verified. "Nick, how much longer will we be staying?"

"I've got some things to do," he said, "and then we should be out of here, probably by tomorrow."

"And where are we going next?"

He grinned at her and said, "Skiing."

THIRTEEN

Nick left Stephanie in her room and went back to his own. He put his suitcase on the bed, opened it, and pried out the false bottom. Using tools and materials secreted there, he turned the room's television into a communications device. It was just one of the ways in which an AXE agent could get in contact with Washington without using conventional means, such as the telephone.

When the TV was transformed, he made contact, and in a few moments he was looking at the face of his boss, David Hawk.

"N3, I've been waiting for you to get in touch. What happened in London? We had reports that you'd disappeared from there without reporting to anyone."

"I had to follow a lead," Nick answered. "I'm in Paris."

"Paris!"

"This is where Lector's trail led me."

"I see. Why haven't you contacted our people there?"

"I'm playing this alone for a while, sir. The contact I had in London was somewhat less than competent."

"I see," Hawk said again. "Are you in any danger?"

"That remains to be seen," Nick said. "Too many people seem to know where I am."

Nick told Hawk about the attempt on his life while he was checking out Lector's last known address.

"Do you think it was our man?" Hawk asked.

"I didn't ask him, sir, but it's possible. I had the 'round peg' on me at the time and I didn't want to risk having it fall into his hands."

"A wise decision."

"Thank you, sir. Uh, sir, before I left Washington, I told you about Howard Clark's daughter approaching me. . . ."

"Yes, yes, what about her?"

"She followed me to London and then here to Paris."

"Without your knowledge?"

"She's getting information from somewhere," Nick said. "She said she found me in London using the DIA computer."

"And Paris?"

" 'Sources,' she said. Could you check with the DIA and find out just what the hell I'm doing in their computer?"

"I will look into it," Hawk said. "Will you be in Paris for the next few days?"

Nick fingered the drawing in his pocket and said, "No, sir. I have reason to believe that Lector might have gone to Switzerland."

"Was he in Paris at all?"

"Yes, staying with a friend, but he left several days ago."

"What makes you think he's in Switzerland?"

"Something he left behind," Nick said, without elaborating on what it was. "And by the way, I think it would be a good idea to find out whether Lector has any friends or relatives living there, someone he might go to."

"I'll work on it, N3."

"I'll check in with you once I'm there."

"When will you be leaving Paris?"

"Immediately, sir. There's no reason for me to stay around here any longer."

"And Miss Clark?"

"I'm taking her along, so I can keep an eye on her."

"I assume you know what you're doing, N3," Hawk said, "so I won't presume to give you my opinion on that. I'll try and have your information for you by the time you get back to me."

"Thank you, sir."

Hawk broke contact without further word, and Nick dismantled his communications device and returned it to the false bottom in his suitcase. Next he picked up the phone and called the desk.

"Henri, this is Mr. Stuart."

"Yes, sir?"

"Prepare my bill, I'll be checking out in a few minutes."

"And the young lady?"

"Yes, her, too. We'll pay you for the other room."

"No need for that, m'sieur," Henri assured him. "Your bill will be ready when you come down."

"Thank you."

He hung up and got himself ready to leave. He debated over the wisdom of taking Stephanie along now that he was no longer sure of her status, but it still made sense to him to have her where he could watch her.

Maybe he'd even let her share a room with him in Switzerland.

He dialed her room and when she answered, he said, "Have you unpacked yet?"

"I haven't had time."

"Good, don't," he told her. "We're leaving. Be ready in five minutes."

"I'm ready now," she said. "But why the change in plans?"

"I'm an impulsive kind of guy," he said, and hung up.

FOURTEEN

They were just able to catch an evening flight to Geneva via Swissair, but they had to go on standby.

On the plane Stephanie asked, "Do you think we'll get a chance to get some skiing in?"

"Hopefully," he answered. "That would mean that this whole business was wrapped up."

"Only if we catch my father's murderer," she added, very seriously.

"Steph—"

"I know, I know, that's not your job."

"Besides that, suppose he's the one who catches us?" Nick proposed.

"I have confidence in you," she said. "If only half of what my father said about you is true, we'll come out on top."

"I appreciate your confidence," he remarked.

The stewardess came by to ask if they wanted drinks. Nick had a bourbon, and Stephanie passed.

At the airport they recovered their bags, went through customs and then outside to grab a cab.

"Why didn't they find your gun?" she asked.

"My suitcase has a false bottom and a special lining that keeps the X-rays from picking it up," he explained.

"Amazing. When your career is over, you could start a new one as a hijacker."

It didn't matter to Nick what hotel they went to, so he virtually left it up to the driver. He just wanted to get into his room and make contact with Hawk.

"God, I'm tired," Stephanie said as they entered the lobby of the hotel.

"Go right to bed when you get to your room, and I'll call you in the morning."

She looked at Nick, but said nothing as he indicated that they would each have their own room. He confirmed it when he asked the clerk to give them connecting rooms. He signed the register Kitty Wills and Nick French.

As the bellboy opened the door to Stephanie's room and carried her luggage in, she giggled.

"What's so funny?" Nick asked.

"Miss Kitty," she said, giggling again.

"What?"

"Gunsmoke," she said, "you know, Marshal Dillon, Miss Kitty?" When Nick didn't reply, she said, "Sorry, but I was a television child."

Nick had never had time for television. It was a waste for him to sit in front of a TV, unless Hawk's face was on it.

The bellboy came over to Stephanie and handed her the key and prepared to show Nick his room.

"Get some sleep," Nick said. "I'll call you in the morning for breakfast."

Looking disappointed, she nodded and said, "All right. Good night."

"Good night."

Nick allowed the bellboy to show him all of the room's features, then tipped him and bade him good night. Alone in the room he debated contacting Hawk now, but he decided to wait until late morning, giving his boss time to come up with the information he had requested.

Nick put his suitcase in a corner, having no intention of

unpacking. The way things were going, they could be there for five minutes or five days.

He walked to the connecting door and listened for a few moments. When he could discern no sound or movement, he tried the knob and found the door locked. He then took a shower, dried off, and lay down on the bed naked with the light on. With his hands cradled behind his head, he thought about everything that had happened over the past few days. Having Stephanie with him saved him the problem of wondering what she was up to, or when she'd pop up. He was still bothered by the fact that she had shown up to begin with, but maybe Hawk would be able to clear that up for him and free his mind for what lay ahead.

Then there was the attempt on his life back in London—God, two countries ago! Was it the courier killer? It was too bad that Nick had not been in a position to try and find that out at the time, but the 'round peg' in his pocket had to take precedence over everything else.

He pulled his jacket over to him and drew the silver tube from the inner breast pocket. Struck again by its resemblance to a cigar tube, he decided to check some smoke shops in the morning and see if he could buy five or six that looked the same. Not a television watcher, Nick had read Poe's *Purloined Letter* and thought he'd apply the idea here.

Replacing the tube in his jacket, he hung it on the bedpost, then retrieved Wilhelmina from his suitcase and tucked her away under his pillow for the night.

"Sleep tight," he told her, and he firmly hoped that she—and he—would.

FIFTEEN

In the morning Nick called Stephanie and asked her to meet him in the hotel dining room for breakfast. She agreed to meet him in a half hour.

Nick went down ahead of her to see if there was a smoke shop or some such shop where he could check out the cigars. When he didn't find one, he asked the bell captain if there was a store nearby where he could buy them. The man gave him directions to a place two blocks away.

He traveled the two blocks, very conscious of his back, but detected no tail. It would have surprised him considerably if he had, since he'd had no idea himself that he was going to be in Switzerland that morning until virtually hours earlier, in Paris.

He found the shop he wanted, and sure enough, they had expensive cigars individually encased in silver tubes exactly like the one he now carried in his pocket. He bought five of them and tucked them into the same pocket with his own. Except for a minute difference in length, they were a perfect match.

He walked back to the hotel and went into the dining room, but Stephanie had not yet come downstairs. He got them a table and ordered coffee while he waited for her to arrive.

Forty-five minutes after he had called her room, Stephanie

walked into the dining room, looking fresh and wide awake.

"You look wonderful," he told her honestly.

"Thank you," she said. "That's the only way a woman can get away with being late all the time, if she puts the time to good use."

"You'll get no complaints from me," he said.

They checked the menu and ordered their breakfasts. Stephanie's was twice the size of Nick's.

"How can you eat that much and not put on any weight?" he asked.

She shrugged and said, "It's just something that I'm able to do."

"It's not going to make you many friends."

"Maybe not, but I enjoy eating," she said. "What are our plans for today?"

"Why don't you go and do some shopping?"

"Shopping?" she said. "That's not what I came here for."

"I know, but we can't do much else until I get some information that I need."

"Why not tell me? Maybe my sources can get it for you faster," she suggested.

"Will you tell me who or what your sources are?" he asked. "Are they DIA sources?"

"Not necessarily."

"All right, look," he said, "why don't you just go and do some shopping, or whatever you want to do, and meet me back here for lunch at, say, one o'clock."

"You're not going to run out on me, are you?" she asked him.

"Of course not."

"I mean, you did it in London; you could very well do it here as well," she reminded him.

"We weren't partners then, right?"

"Right, but I don't really feel like an equal partner," she

complained. "There are things you're keeping from me."

"Oh?" he replied. "And there's nothing that you're keeping from me, I suppose?"

She frowned a moment and then said, "Why don't we meet back here for lunch at, say, one o'clock?"

"Wonderful idea!"

SIXTEEN

After breakfast, Stephanie left the hotel, but that was no guarantee that she wouldn't turn right around and come back again and go to her room. Nick went up to his room, picked the lock on the connecting door, and left it ajar. After that, he went about transforming the TV, and in moments he was staring at Hawk's face in living color.

"N3."

"Sir, did you get that information I asked you for?"

"On Dr. Lector, yes. He has two friends in Switzerland. One lives in Geneva and one just outside. You'll have to check both."

"Naturally."

Hawk threw Nick a look, then went on. He gave him the addresses of both friends and the correct spellings of their names.

"What about the information on the DIA?"

"That is a little more difficult. The DIA computers are not open to us."

"I didn't think you'd get information out of them willingly, but wasn't there some way our machines could tap into theirs?"

"We're still working on it."

"But if a mere file clerk can do it, why can't AXE?"

"We are working on it, N3."

"I realize that."

"Concentrate on the task at hand then."

"Yes, sir, I will."

"Then get on with it. Find Dr. Lector and make your delivery. After you've done that, we can worry about why the DIA computer was able to locate you."

"Yes, sir. Is there anything else you can tell me? Have there been any leads on the doctor's whereabouts?"

"None. Your guess is as good as ours."

"Well, that's what I'm working on, sir. A guess . . . All right, I'll keep in touch."

"Do that," Hawk said, and he broke the connection.

Nick disassembled his communications device and replaced it in his suitcase, then checked Stephanie's room and found it still empty. He closed and relocked the connecting door, and then left his room.

A guess, that's what it was all right. Just because a man drew a picture of a chalet that reminded a young girl of a place she'd been to before did not necessarily mean he was planning a trip to Switzerland, although Stephanie did say the chalet was one of Switzerland's most famous. But Stephanie herself was still a question mark in his mind. For all Nick knew, Lector could have been in Vail, Colorado, or even Bear Mountain, New York! Still, there was the fact that Lector had two close friends here in Switzerland.

The obvious one to check first would be the one who lived right there in the city. He'd have to rent a car for the other.

He caught a cab in front of the hotel and gave him the address Hawk had given him.

After a few miles, Nick noticed that the address was in the oldest section of the city. There were no new structures here, just old one-story and two-story homes, and the cab now pulled up in front of one.

The man he was looking for was Carl Kaufman, and the man's name was right on the door of the two-story house he was standing in front of. Nick ascended the steps and rang the bell. He waited a few moments, but there was no answer. He rang again, and when there was still no answer, he took out his lock picks and let himself in. With a last look at the empty street, Nick pushed the door in and entered.

After closing the door behind him, he stood stock still, and then withdrew Wilhelmina from her holster. The tension that was in the area was almost physical, especially to a man with Nick Carter's instincts.

He was standing in a small foyer with a stairway ahead of him and rooms to the right and left. Although it was daylight outside, inside it was dim, almost dark, and it was as quiet as death.

Which was what he was afraid of.

Obviously, someone had gotten there ahead of him, unless his instincts were totally off the track this time, which was not likely.

Nick stayed where he was and kept his ears wide open, listening for telltale footsteps or creaking floorboards, but if there was someone else in the house with him, that person was a professional.

But what was that person doing there? And how had he known that Nick was coming there? He himself hadn't known until only moments ago.

This was another case of someone knowing his moves—perhaps even before he did, this time.

No time to think about it now; he'd kick it around later. Right now he was in a very dangerous situation, and perhaps the thing to do was to turn around and walk right out again; but as long as there was a chance that he would find Carl Kaufman, or even Anton Lector himself, he had to stay and see this through.

In addition to the rooms on his right and left, there seemed to be a room further down at the end of the hall and past the staircase; it was probably the kitchen. Upstairs had to be the bedroom or bedrooms. Nick had to make a decision now, and that was which way to go. Check the rooms out down here, or go right up the steps to the second floor? In any one of those rooms there could have been someone lying in wait for him, whether it be the courier killer or not.

Nick opted for the upstairs. If Lector was or had been there, he would have been staying in a guest room of some sort, and that would have been upstairs.

Moving slowly, he started forward, wary of the two doors on either side of him, as he approached the stairs. When he reached them, he started up, moving sideways so that he could keep his eye on upstairs as well as downstairs.

Nick used his eyes *and* ears as he ascended the steps, and when he reached the top, he found a hallway that extended to his left. On his right was an open door. When he looked inside, he found a small bathroom in which no one would be able to hide.

Moving to his left, with his gun ready, he kept his back against the wall and kept an eye on the stairs he had just walked up.

As Nick went further down the hall, he became aware of an odor in the air, an odor he had encountered before and was able to identify.

The smell of blood.

The odor was coming from the first room he reached, and he moved into the room sideways, keeping his gun extended ahead of him. He saw the body from the doorway, but remained where he was rather than rushing in. He executed two quick steps, which brought him into the room, then swung the door closed in case there was someone behind it. When he saw that there wasn't, he closed the door all the way so that he'd have some kind of advance warning if someone wanted to come in after him.

Before looking at the dead man, he went over to the closet and pulled it open. It was empty. Convinced that no one else was in the room, he finally moved to the body.

There were no pictures available of Anton Lector, but Nick had been given a full description of the doctor, and the man on the floor with his throat cut was not Lector. He therefore had to be the doctor's friend, Carl Kaufman.

Kaufman's face was a frozen mask of terror, and his eyes, though open, were glazed over. Why had he been killed, Nick wondered. Coincidence was out of the question; things had gone much too far to even consider that. But what was the point of killing this man? And the fact that he was dead did not have to mean that Lector had even been there. That was still to be checked out, hopefully in the next few moments.

Nick closed the dead man's eyes and rose to his feet, still holding his gun ready. He moved to the door and snapped it open. He rushed into the hall, going down to one knee, swinging his gun to cover both ends. Satisfied that no one was stalking him on the second floor, he moved down to the end of the hall to check out the remaining room.

Using the same care he had exhibited since entering the house, he moved into the other room and checked behind the door before closing it tight. That done, he moved to the single closet in the room and satisfied himself that it was empty. Feeling fairly secure, he moved about the room, examining it in the same manner he had examined the guest room in the LaMouche house. There was no writing desk in this room, but there was a trash bucket, and he checked that as well. When he was done, he had found no indication that Anton Lector had ever been there, which made the death of Carl Kaufman even more puzzling.

If Lector wasn't there now and had never been there, why had Kaufman been killed? Where was the purpose in that?

Nick walked to the window and looked out at the empty street. He hadn't heard a door open, but suddenly there was a man below him walking away from the house. He had to have come from inside the house.

Nick opened the window and tried to do it quietly, but it was old, and as he pushed it up, it made a loud, squeaking sound, made even louder by the fact that the street was quiet. The man on the ground looked up, saw Nick in the window, then raised his hand, snapping off a shot as he took off down the street.

The bullet went through the window and shattered it. Nick quickly swung his legs over the windowsill and dropped to the ground with bone-jarring force. He took off in hot pursuit.

The man had a fair headstart, but he was still in sight down the street, running hard. Nick didn't know if he'd be able to catch him, but he had to try. If this was the courier killer, the shoe was on the other foot this time, and it was Nick who was the pursuer. Obviously, if the man didn't have things his own way, he preferred to leave it for another time. This time, Nick wanted to press the issue, even though he still had that silver tube on him.

The fleeing man turned a corner and it took Nick precious seconds to reach the same corner. For a moment he lost sight of the man, but then spotted him again. The distance between them had increased and Nick tried to close that distance by speeding up.

Nick suddenly became aware of the sound of a siren, but couldn't tell from which direction it was coming. He found out soon enough. He was about to cross the same intersection his quarry had just crossed when a small police car came out of one of the sidestreets and blocked it. Several uniformed men jumped out of the car with their guns drawn.

The first thing they saw was Nick Carter running toward them with a gun in his hand.

"Stop!" one of them shouted in English, as if he could tell just from looking at Nick that he was an American.

It didn't take Nick more than a second to decide what his

safest course of action would be. He stopped running and threw his hands into the air, holding his gun high above his head.

As the police officers approached him, he tried to explain what the situation was, but all they knew was that they had caught a man running down the street with a gun in his hand as they were responding to a report of a murder.

Nick knew he was lucky they hadn't fired at him on sight. They took his gun, handcuffed him, and deposited him in the back seat of their car.

He couldn't help thinking that he was going to be late meeting Stephanie for lunch.

SEVENTEEN

They took Nick to the police station but did not process or fingerprint him right away. Instead, they put him in a room with two chairs and a table, locked the door, and left him there for a good two hours. During that time, Nick pieced together what must have happened. While he was checking the upstairs of the house, the other man must have called the police, hoping that Nick would be picked up for the murder.

Why? If the man was the courier killer, why would he want Nick in a Swiss jail? How could he have access to him there? Maybe the point of killing all the couriers over the past few months had nothing to do with what they were carrying. Maybe having Nick executed by Swiss justice was just as good.

His train of thought was broken when he heard the lock click open on the door. He expected to be taken from the room and moved somewhere else, but instead a short man with graying dark hair and a slight paunch walked in and shut the door behind him. He was holding Nick's wallet, which had been taken from him earlier.

Holding the wallet up next to his ear—as if it had some great secret to tell him—the man said, "You are American."

"That's not hard to tell."

"You have remarkably little identification in your wallet, Mr.—"

"French, Nick French."

"Mr. French," the man repeated. "I am Superintendent Rheiner, Otto Wilhelm Rheiner, at your service."

"The only thing you can do for me, Mr. Rheiner, is get me out of here."

"In due time," the superintendent said. He dropped Nick's wallet on the table, clasped his hands behind his back, and began to walk around the room, disappearing from Nick's sight for about five seconds at a time.

"Do you know a man named Carl Kaufman, Mr. French?"

"I do not," Nick said, without hesitation.

"But you were at his home earlier today."

"Was I?"

"I believe so, yes," Rheiner said.

"If you say so."

"What were you doing when my officers saw you?"

"Running."

Rheiner chuckled and said, "You Americans. Could you be a little more specific—or would that be against your American sense of humor?"

"I was chasing someone."

"Indeed? Who?"

"A man."

"Is that more of your sense—"

"That's all I know," Nick broke in. "I never saw his face, and probably wouldn't have known him if I had."

"I see. And why were you chasing him with a gun?"

"He came out of Carl Kaufman's house and took a shot at me," Nick explained, actually telling the truth.

"But you said you didn't know Carl Kaufman?" Rheiner reminded him.

"That's right, I don't," Nick said. "And from the way I've been treated and the way you're talking, I guess I never will."

Rheiner stopped circling Nick and stood in front of him, smiling. He said, "Very perceptive of you, Mr. French. You're quite right, Mr. Kaufman is dead. He was shot."

"I see," Nick said, not reacting to the lie. "And I suppose you've checked the bullet against my gun?"

"Yes," Rheiner said, "and it matched."

"In that case, I guess I'd better speak to someone from my consulate."

Rheiner studied Nick for a few moments, then said, "That may not be necessary, Mr. French. I lied."

"About what?"

"Carl Kaufman was not shot; his throat was cut."

"Oh," Nick said. "Then what am I doing here?"

"What were you doing there?" the superintendent asked.

"Someone from the United States asked me to look him up when I got here. I was to say hello."

"With a gun?"

Nick tried to look chagrined and said, "That's just a bad habit, I guess."

"Indeed, I would say," Rheiner agreed. "We frown on visitors running down our streets with guns, Mr. French."

"I don't blame you," Nick said, "but I wasn't the only one."

"No, you were not," the other man said. "My men said that they did see another man, but could not tell whether he was carrying a weapon or not. On the other hand, they quite clearly saw the gun in your hand. They thought it wiser to stop you than to chase him."

"Maybe they made a mistake," Nick suggested.

"Perhaps."

"What do we do now?"

"Well, you were being held for questioning," the policeman said. "I have questioned you."

"Am I free to go?"

"Not quite. You can leave here, but please stay in the city."

Nick stood up and said, "I'm supposed to visit someone else, as well."

"Where do they live, please?"

Nick gave him the address and the man nodded.

"It is just outside the city, but I will allow it—uh, as long as this person does not end up dead, as well."

"I hope not," Nick said, picking up his wallet.

"You may count your money, if you wish. It is all there."

"I'll trust you," Nick said, tucking the wallet away. "I would like my cigars back, though, if it's no trouble."

"I don't think it will be," Rheiner said. He reached into his jacket and brought out Nick's cigars. When he handed them to Nick, there were only five, and Nick's heart began to beat a little faster.

"I had six," Nick said.

"Really?" Rheiner asked, frowning. He seemed to count the silver tubes in Nick's hand and then said, "It would appear you only have five now."

"That's right."

"Well," the man said, "perhaps you smoked one and do not remember."

Nick examined the man for a few moments, then nodded and said, "Perhaps," tucking the tubes away in his own jacket. He did not want to pay too much attention to the matter, or to the five tubes he now had, until he was away from the police station.

"What about my gun?"

"Ah, I am afraid I will have to hold onto that."

"Why?"

"I see no reason for you to have to carry a gun in my country, Mr. French. Can you give me one?"

"Not one that would satisfy you," Nick said.

"You see? I am compelled to hold onto it."

"Will it be returned when I leave?"

"That I could not say. Why do you carry a gun in the first place, may I ask?"

"Protection," Nick said.

"From what?"

"People, like the one who killed Carl Kaufman."

"Your logic is somewhat erratic, I think, but I will not pursue the matter. Check with me if you intend to leave the city, and we will discuss the matter then, eh?"

"Sure."

Rheiner stepped back and ushered Nick to the door. When they were outside the room, he pointed and said, "You may go out that way—and please remember what I said about not leaving without checking with me first."

"I'll remember, Superintendent Rheiner," Nick promised.

Nick left the station, but waited until he was out of sight before he removed the cigar cases from his pocket. He breathed a sigh of relief when he saw that one of them was slightly longer than the rest and that the seals on all five were unbroken. Apparently, whoever had taken the other one had enjoyed one good smoke.

Nick's next problem was Wilhelmina and how to get her back. He felt naked without her, and if push came to shove with the courier killer, Hugo wouldn't be enough.

He grabbed a cab and told the driver to take him to the American consulate.

EIGHTEEN

The man Nick was taken to see at the consulate claimed to be an undersecretary of something or other, but Nick had other ideas.

So, it seemed, did Superintendent Rheiner.

"The superintendent called here when they picked you up," the man said. His name was David Manners and although he *was* technically an undersecretary—of something or other—his real job was known only to himself and an office in Virginia.

"He wanted to know what the American CIA was doing in his city," Manners explained.

"CIA?" Nick asked.

"That's right," Manners said. "You're not CIA, are you, Mr. . . . French?"

"No."

"You're not a tourist, either."

"No, I'm not."

"Then who are you?"

"I don't know what your real position is, Manners, or what your clearance is, but call this number," Nick said, taking pencil and paper from the man's desk and writing down a Washington, D.C., phone number. "And then get me my gun back."

"Just like that?" Manners asked, picking up the phone number.

"Just like that. Call me at my hotel and let me know what happens," Nick said, and left without further discussion.

Catching another cab, he went back to his hotel to look for Stephanie so he could explain his whereabouts. By now she must have been convinced that he had run out on her. If the shoe had been on the other foot, he would have had the same thoughts.

Maybe she'd let him explain over dinner.

NINETEEN

Nick went straight to his room and knocked on the connecting door. When there was no answer, he cursed out loud. He was hungry and would have rather gone right to dinner than have to go looking for her. He left the door unlocked and went to take a shower before starting his search.

When he came out of the bathroom, he found her sitting on his bed.

"You bastard!"

"Sit down, Stephanie, and I'll explain."

"Explain leaving me sitting in the dining room for a couple of hours, telling myself that you hadn't run out on me."

"But I haven't."

"How was I supposed to know that?"

"You know it now."

"Yeah, now!"

"So why are you so mad?"

She pouted a bit, but finally said, "I was worried about you, you sonofabitch. I thought maybe somebody killed you."

"No, but somebody tried."

"What do you mean?"

"Let me get dressed," he told her. "We'll go to dinner and I'll tell you everything."

"I'll change," she said, then added, "but I'm leaving the

door open so you can't disappear again.''

''I don't have any intention of doing that,'' he said.

She stood up, then covered her mouth and giggled.

''Did you know that you were naked?''

He smiled and said, ''Actually, I was hoping you'd notice that.''

''Oh,'' she said, approaching him. ''I noticed.''

When her hands got busy, he said, ''How would you feel about a late dinner?''

As an answer, her hands got even busier, and he thought he might as well get busy, too.

They had dinner in the hotel dining room where he filled her in on all that had happened that day. He left out the part about going to the consulate and trying to get his gun back.

''God, you're lucky they didn't shoot you down in the street,'' she said.

''Yeah, I've thought about that once or twice,'' he said, ''especially while I was sitting in that room.''

Over dessert, she asked, ''So what's on our agenda tomorrow?''

''I—we've—got another man to go and see.''

''Is he going to be dead, too?''

''I certainly hope not,'' he said, signaling to the waiter for the check.

''What if he is?''

He frowned at her. ''Let's worry about that tomorrow, shall we? Why ruin tonight?''

''Oh?'' she asked. ''Have you got plans for tonight?''

He signed the check and stood up.

''I thought maybe a nightcap in one of our rooms.''

''Which one?''

''Yours.''

''Why, all of a sudden?'' she asked, then added, ''Not that I mind, of course.''

"Well, to tell you the truth," he said as they headed for the elevator, "since I don't have my gun to sleep with tonight . . ."

"You stink!" she said.

TWENTY

In the morning they had breakfast in Stephanie's room and then Nick went through the connecting door to his own room to shower and dress while she did the same.

"What now?" she asked in the hall.

"Now we've got to rent a car and get directions to this address," he said.

"What address?"

"This one," he said, tapping his temple. "Come on—and stop asking me 'what now?' all the time. Just follow my lead. We'll never get anywhere if I have to stop and explain every move to you before we make it."

"Well, at least you said 'we.' "

"We're partners, aren't we?"

"Maybe I'm starting to believe that," she said.

Nick asked the clerk where the nearest car rental agency was, and the clerk gave him directions.

"We can walk," he told Stephanie.

"Great."

Nick had a few anxious moments when they walked out of the hotel. The courier killer could have opened fire on them at that moment and Nick would've had no gun with which to return fire. It might've meant their lives.

It was then that he remembered the little .25 in Stephanie's purse. It wasn't much, and it wouldn't be much use from across the street, but it was better than having Hugo alone.

"Did you clear it with the police so you could leave the city?" she asked.

"It's all taken care of, Stephanie."

"What if he hadn't thought you were a CIA agent, Nick?"

He looked up at the sky and said, "I probably wouldn't have seen the light of day for quite a while."

"And I would've thought that you had really run out on me."

"See?" he said. "I would have been in jail and had you mad at me at the same time. I don't know which would have been worse."

"I do," she said, and dug at his ribs with an elbow.

They rented a little Audi and Nick got in behind the wheel. Stephanie climbed in the front seat next to him. "Let's go," she said.

Nick had gotten directions from the girl behind the counter at the rental agency, and they had about an hour's drive ahead of them. Nick kept checking the rear-view mirror to see if they were being followed, but what he really worried about was somebody—the killer?—getting there ahead of him. Only how would that somebody know where he was going?

Worry about that later, Hawk had said, but he couldn't. He had to worry about it now. Things were getting too hot.

"You keep looking in the rear-view mirror," Stephanie said, twisting around in her seat.

"Force of habit," Nick said, dismissing it.

"What a way to live."

"Your father lived the same way," he reminded her.

"And died," she retorted, and that killed conversation for quite a while.

After some miles and almost twenty minutes, Stephanie said, "How much further?"

"Shouldn't be too long now."

She lapsed into silence again, arms folded in front of her and eyes straight ahead.

There was a long stretch of road where there were no buildings or structures of any kind.

"Great place for an ambush," Stephanie said.

"Not so loud," he warned.

Finally, small houses began to appear at intervals, and then they came into a small village.

"This is it," he said. "Now we just have to find the right street."

Before they could do that, they had to stop at a small pastry shop and ask how to get there. The man behind the counter smiled and gave them exact directions. As they were leaving he said, "Gustav Balnap must be a very popular man, these days."

Nick stopped short and turned back to the man.

"Why do you say that?"

"You are the second person to ask for directions to his home in the past hour."

"I see. And what did this other person look like?"

"A man" was the answer, along with a shrug.

"Alone?"

"Oh yes, quite alone."

"Thank you."

Nick hurried out to the car and got it started with a jerk.

"What's the matter?"

"Someone else is an hour ahead of us."

"Who?"

"A man. Do you have your gun with you?"

"My gun?" she asked. "How do you know I have a—"

"Who do you think cleaned it for you?"

She opened her purse and looked at the gun, then looked back at Nick with a frown.

"I have it," she said.

"Do you know how to use it?"

''Probably not as well as you.''

''Give it here, then,'' he said, taking his left hand from the wheel and extending it toward her. After a slight hesitation, he felt her lay the automatic in his hand, and he was struck by how light it felt, like a toy.

A deadly toy.

At least he hoped it was deadly.

TWENTY-ONE

"A farm?" Stephanie asked.

"That's what it looks like," Nick said.

He had to stop the car to get out and open a gate that would admit them to the grounds.

"Be careful," she told him.

He kept the little .25 in his left hand, small enough to be completely hidden there, and then used his right to unhook the gate and swing it inward. When he got back into the car, he kept the gun in his hand and drove through the gate.

"You're really worried about this, aren't you?" she asked.

"Let's just say that I wish you weren't here, and I wish I had my own gun back."

"Great," she said, hugging her arms.

"Just stay in the car, Stephanie—"

"Oh no, Nick," she cut in. "I think the safest place for me is with you."

"All right, but you've got to do exactly as I say."

"You got it."

Nick pulled the car up in front of the farmhouse, which was small and old, but had been kept up by someone who cared. However, the barn was in a state of disrepair, possibly because the owner, Gustav Belnap, couldn't afford to fix it.

"What do we do—" she started to ask, but remembered

that he'd asked her not to ask that question. "Never mind."

"Just follow me," he said, "and if anything happens to me, run like hell."

"Shit," she said in a whisper.

"Let's go."

When they got out of the car, Nick switched the gun from his left hand to his right.

"Try the door," he said as they mounted the front porch. He studied the grounds, paying special attention to the barn, but there was no movement to be seen.

"Uh-oh," she said.

"What?"

"The door's open," she said. "That's bad, isn't it?"

"That remains to be seen," he said. "Step back and let me go in first."

"Maybe we should get some help."

"Like who?" he said. "Just do what I tell you, Stephanie, and everything will be fine."

"All right, all right."

He pushed the door open and slipped in, holding the toy cannon at the ready.

"Nick?" Stephanie whispered from outside.

He was going to shush her, then realized how futile and silly that would probably be, but if he didn't answer her, she'd just keep calling. He stuck his left hand out the door so she would take it, and then drew her in next to him when she did.

"Quiet," he told her, and she nodded.

He inspected the inside of the farmhouse, which was in semidarkness. Just like the home of Carl Kaufman. He had the distinct feeling he was about to relive the incident all over again.

"What's the matter?"

"If this is like last time—" he started to say, and then stopped. He moved toward the door and looked out. "He's in the barn."

"How do you know? And who is in the barn?"

"The killer. When I was at Kaufman's house, he let me go upstairs and he stayed downstairs."

"This house doesn't have an upstairs."

"Right, so he'll stay in the barn while we're in the house."

"What about the man who lives here?"

"If he was here when the killer got here, then I think he's dead."

"But we haven't checked all of the rooms."

"I'll do that now. You stay here by the door. Here," he said, giving her the gun.

"What do I do if he comes out of the barn?"

"If he comes toward the house, shoot him, but let him get close first. That popgun won't be much good unless he's close."

"All—all right," she said a little shakily.

"I won't be long," he promised.

He moved further into the house and picked out the two doorways that led into other rooms. Any other doors were either closets or bathrooms.

He found the remains of Gustav Balnap in the second bedroom. In the first, he found pieces of paper in the trash bucket with drawings on them. He pocketed them and went back to the door where Stephanie was nervously peering out.

"What—"

"I found somebody," he said. "It must be Gustav."

"Dead?"

He nodded. "Like Kaufman, his throat was cut."

She looked at his face then and stammered. "Is . . . is that how—"

"Yes, Stephanie, that's how your father was killed."

"Then this killer you're referring to is the man who killed my father?"

"Yes."

"Then your assignment is the same thing as . . . as looking for my father's murderer."

"Not exactly," he said. "What I'm doing is waiting for your father's killer to find me."

"Why didn't you tell me? Why'd you let me say all those nasty things to you in Washington?"

"You needed to blow off steam," he told her. "Besides, it was none of your business."

"Now that's debatable," she said.

"It might be debatable," he agreed, "but not now."

He took the gun from her and she said, "I know you said not to ask, but what are you going to do now?"

"I'm going over to the barn to meet our friend," he said. He took two steps out the door and then there was a shot; a bullet plowed into the wood frame around the door.

Stephanie shouted and Nick leaped back through the door into the safety of the house.

"Are you all right?" he asked her.

"Yes, I think so," she replied. "How about you?"

"I'm fine," he said, picking himself up from the floor. "What did you yell for?"

"I got scared," she said sheepishly.

He moved back to the door and peered out.

"Are you going to shoot back?" she asked.

"With this?" he asked, indicating her little .25, which looked pitifully small in his hand.

"Well, what's he got?"

"Probably a rifle of some kind."

"So we're stuck?"

"No," Nick said. "I'll draw his fire and you run for the car and get out of here."

"Oh, no—"

"Oh, yes."

"I'm not leaving you, Nick," she said firmly.

"Give me one good reason why not, and you can stay."

She spent a few moments trying to think of a good excuse, and finally said, "If I leave and you get killed, I'll probably never get my gun back."

He stared at her for a few beats. then shrugged his shoulders and said, "Stay put, then. I'll make a run for the car."

"Nick!"

"I'm not going to leave," he added hurriedly. "I'll get in the car and drive it into the barn. Maybe I can flush him out, or get close enough to use this peashooter of yours."

"Guns have feelings too," she warned.

"You're nuts. Stay here, okay?"

"It's not going to be easy," she said. Nick stuck his head out to take another look and another bullet plowed into the side of the house. "I take that back," she said.

"Just do it," he said, "and wish me luck."

She kissed him on the cheek and said, "Good luck, Nick."

He got ready to spring out the door, then had second thoughts as he asked her, "Did you lock the door on your side?"

"No, why?"

"I locked mine," he said, and took off.

He ran for the car, which meant he had to cross about twenty feet of open ground. He heard the shots and actually felt one bury itself in the dirt behind his right heel. When he reached the little car, he knew that the driver's side was locked, so he vaulted over the roof, and as he landed, a bullet went through the front windshield on the passenger side.

Nick yanked the door open and threw himself onto the front seat; the key was still in the ignition. Switching the gun to his left hand, he started the car, put it into drive, and floored the gas pedal.

He was hoping that the killer was on the ground floor, where he'd have to move to avoid the car. If he was up in the hayloft, he'd be free to take pot shots.

As the car approached the barn, Nick caught sight of the man behind one of the barn doors. In seconds he was gone, and the car broke through into the barn, striking the one closed door, not only knocking it open, but off one hinge, as well.

Inside the barn, Nick turned the wheel hard and the car did a quick one-hundred-and-eighty-degree turn. Without turning off the motor, Nick slid over to the passenger side, pushed the door open, and tumbled out.

The only sound in the barn was that of the car's running motor. Nick sat with his back against the car, Stephanie's gun in his right hand. In the enclosed area of the barn, the gun suddenly became more of a weapon and less of a toy. He looked above at the hayloft, hoping that the killer hadn't had time to get up there. But if his instincts were right, his rented car was now between himself and the killer.

Moving up on his haunches, he eased down toward the front of the car so that he was up against a tire. That way he would be less of a target from underneath the car. He held the gun ready, counted to three, and then stood up and braced himself on the hood of the car with the gun held out in front of him.

One of the barn doors was hanging by one hinge and was still swaying from the force of Nick's entry. Scanning the wall opposite him, he saw that there wasn't anyplace to hide; yet the man who had been shooting at them was nowhere in sight.

Had he gotten out of the barn immediately after Nick's entry?

If he had, he was either long gone, or he'd gone to the house, in which case he now had Stephanie. Nick was too much of a pro to let that thought send him rushing out from his cover. Until he proved otherwise, he was going to act on the assumption that the killer was still there in the barn with him.

Slowly, holding the gun out in front of him, he began to move out from behind the car, which was quickly filling the air inside the barn with carbon monoxide. There were too many holes in the structure of the barn—not to mention the open door—for it to be deadly, but it was becoming uncomfortable.

Nick made a slow circuit of the barn with his eyes, spotting no one. There were two alternatives. Either the killer was in the hayloft or he was behind the door that was hanging on one hinge, waiting for his chance.

Nick didn't think he was in the hayloft. He was sure he'd seen the man at the door, and he hadn't had time to run up the ladder before Nick drove into the barn.

He had to be behind the door, waiting. If Nick approached the door to pull it shut, the killer could shoot him easily. Firing his own gun through the door was too chancy. He could use up his ammunition and not even hit the man. And he wasn't too sure the .25 had the power to penetrate the door.

What he had to do was decoy the man into pushing the door shut himself.

The ladder to the hayloft was made of wood, and it appeared to be unstable. If a man tried to climb it, it would surely rattle and make noise. Nick backed his way up to it, keeping his front covered. Reaching behind him, he stopped when he encountered the ladder with his left hand and then, tightening his grip on the gun, he rattled the ladder, hoping that it would sound as if he were climbing it.

As the ladder rattled, the door suddenly swung shut, propelled by the power of a kick. The killer, after standing with his back to the wall for so long, stepped forward and pointed his rifle at the ladder, where he apparently hoped to find Nick's back. Instead, he saw Nick standing there, pointing a gun at him. Nick saw the shock on the man's face as he pulled the trigger on the .25 four times. Each of his four shots struck the man in the chest, and after the fourth shot, the man's hands opened and the rifle fell to the ground. He opened his mouth as if he were going to try and say something, but no sound came out, and then he fell forward onto his face.

TWENTY-TWO

As Nick approached the body, he kicked the rifle away, but then he heard someone coming up behind him. He turned quickly with the gun pointed.

"Wait!" Stephanie shouted. "It's me!" She had her hands up in front of her to protect herself.

"I told you to stay put."

"I heard shooting," she said, then added, "at least I think it was shooting. It sounded so faint."

"That's what this popgun sounds like from where you were," he said. He turned back to the fallen man and crouched down next to him.

"Is that him?" she asked.

"It's somebody," he said, checking first to make sure the man was dead, and then going through his pockets for identification. He felt sure, though, that whatever I.D. the man had on him would be false.

"Who?"

"According to this I.D., his name was Eric Rauter," Nick said, reading the contents of the man's wallet.

"You don't believe it?"

"Stephanie, I have identification that says I'm Nick French—and a few others, as well."

"Dumb question, huh?"

He didn't answer. He searched the man further, but

couldn't find anything of importance.

"Is he the man you saw running from Carl Kaufman's house?" she asked.

"I can't be sure," he answered. "I never saw that man's face."

"So we don't know if this is the man you've been looking for," she said, "the man who killed my father."

"The man I'm looking for is someone else entirely," he reminded her, standing up. "But I know what you mean, and, no, I can't be sure. Who else could he be, though? He's certainly not a farmer."

"Should we call somebody?"

"Like who?"

"The police?"

He shook his head.

"The last thing I need is to end up in the hands of the police again," he said. "No, I'll make a phone call when we get back to the hotel and get a cleanup crew out here."

"A cleanup crew?"

"Yes. Maybe we can find out who this guy is after all. He might tell us more dead than he would have alive."

"And what about the man you're looking for?"

Nick touched his pocket and said, "He was here, I know that much. He left some more pictures behind."

"Let me see."

"Not now. Let's get out of here first before someone comes along. As it is, a couple of people know we were coming to this place. The faster we get our people out here to clean up, the better off we'll be."

"I'm for that," she said. "Was the car damaged?"

He turned to look at it.

"Just a bullet hole in the front windshield. We'll drive it to the outskirts of town and then leave it. The rental agency will find it sooner or later, and by that time we'll be gone. We can't afford to take the time to answer questions about bullet holes."

He started for the car and then stopped when he realized that she wasn't following. He turned and saw her staring down at the body.

"Stephanie?"

"I should be feeling something," she said. "If this is the man who killed my father, I should be feeling—"

"Maybe the key word here is 'if,' " he proposed.

"What do you mean?" she asked, tearing her eyes away from the dead man.

"Let's talk about it back at the hotel, Stephanie," he said. "Come on. We don't have any time to waste."

"All right," she said. She took one last look at the dead man, then said again, "All right," and followed Nick to the car.

TWENTY-THREE

When they got back to the hotel after ditching the car and catching a bus, it was already early evening.

"Why don't we have dinner in our rooms, and then we can talk," Nick suggested at her door.

"I'd like to take a shower first."

"I'll go to my room and order. The connecting door will be unlocked. Come in when you're ready."

She nodded and went into her room. He walked down the hall and let himself into his own room.

He called room service and ordered dinner for two, then undressed to take a shower. As he soaped himself, he wondered why he always seemed to be a step behind Lector, while the killer was always a step ahead. Now it should be easier, he thought. Without the killer hovering about, waiting to strike, it should be much simpler to track down Dr. Lector.

If, indeed, the killer was dead.

That nagged at him as he dressed. Was the man he killed the "courier killer," as he had come to think of him? This was a new question to gnaw at him, along with wondering how the man had always managed to stay ahead of him.

Before the food arrived, along with Stephanie, he made a call to the American consulate and asked for Manners.

"Can we talk freely?" he asked as Manners came on the line.

Manners made no pretense about not knowing what Nick was talking about.

"This line is clean," he said without hesitation.

"There's been a problem," Nick said. "I need a cleanup crew and an identification." He gave Manners the address, but did not go into specific detail about what had happened, even though the man had assured him it was safe to talk.

"All right," Manners said. He did not sound happy to have Nick in his city, but he had obviously checked up on him.

"I don't care if the crew is yours or mine," Nick said.

"I'll take care of it."

"Fine."

"When can you come in . . . so we can talk?"

"I don't know," Nick said. "There are some other things—"

"I've recovered that item you wanted," Manners said, meaning Wilhelmina.

'I'll make a point of coming in tomorrow," Nick said. "Hopefully, you'll also have that other information for me."

"I'll try."

"Until tomorrow, then," Nick said, and hung up.

As he hung up, there was a knock on his door. He opened it and permitted the bellboy to wheel in the tray with dinner on it.

"Thank you," he said, tipping the man and ushering him out. Then he walked to the connecting door and knocked on it, just to let Stephanie know that the soup was on.

He had everything set by the time she opened the door and walked in, wearing a robe.

"I hope you don't mind the informal attire," she said.

"Not at all," he smiled.

She gave him a halfhearted smile in return and sat down at the tray opposite him.

"Are you all right?" he asked.

"I think so," she said. "I think I just need to talk."

"Let's talk, then," he said.

"What do I do if that man is the one who killed my father?"

"You go home," he said. "You go back to your job at the DIA."

"As a file clerk?" she said, making a face. "I don't think I could do that."

"Go home anyway. Change your job, but go home."

"And what if he's not the man who killed my father?"

"How are you going to be sure, either way?"

"By staying with you."

"Stephanie—"

"By seeing your assignment through to the end. If you succeed, and there are no more attempts on your life, then I'll be sure—but not until then."

"You've thought about this?"

"As much as I could," she said. "I've made my decision; now I have to wait for you to make yours."

"You mean I have a choice in the matter?" he asked.

She knew he was referring to the way she had dogged him to London and Paris, and she smiled genuinely this time.

"Yes," she said, "this time."

TWENTY-FOUR

After dinner, they skipped dessert and decided to go straight to bed. When Stephanie dropped her robe, revealing nothing underneath, Nick responded in kind. And for the rest of the evening they made slow and easy love. They hadn't skipped dessert after all.

Early in the morning, Nick sent Stephanie back to her own room, but first he gave her back her gun.

"I don't want you complaining that I didn't give it back to you," he said, so that she wouldn't assume he was giving it to her for another reason.

When she left his room, he showered, dressed, and then left to go to the consulate. He told her to have breakfast in her room and that he'd be back for lunch.

"Hopefully," she said.

"I'd have to be arrested to keep me from coming back," he said.

"Don't even say that in jest."

He caught a cab in front of the hotel and told the driver to take him to the American consulate. He got in to see Manners much faster this time than the last.

"Manners," he said by way of greeting as he entered the office.

"I haven't been told very much about you, Carter, except that I'm to cooperate."

"They told you my name, too, I see."

"And not a hell of a lot else," the man replied sourly. He opened a drawer in his desk and brought out a large brown envelope, which contained something bulky, and handed it to Nick.

It was Wilhelmina.

Nick took the gun out of the envelope, checked it out to make sure it hadn't been damaged, or fired, and then tucked it away in his empty holster.

He felt whole again.

"Sit down," Manners invited, though it didn't sound very much like an invitation. Nick sat.

"Took care of that cleanup job last night, but we're going to have to tell the police something. Can't have a farmer just drop out of sight without questions being asked."

"I'll be gone, so I don't care what you tell them," Nick said.

"Sure," Manners said, putting a bit of bitterness into that one word. He was about forty or so and a little heavy, which probably came from sitting behind a desk.

"Ever work the field, Manners?"

"I did," he replied. "I'm not here by choice."

"I sympathize," Nick said, "but don't take it out on me. I didn't put you here."

Manners caught Nick's eyes and held them for a while, then nodded curtly and said, "Fair enough."

"Did you tell the superintendent that I'm not CIA?"

"We're letting him think what he wants. He always does, anyway. Don't worry, we can handle him."

Nick touched his gun through his jacket and said, "Obviously. What did you find out about the man I killed?"

"He's nothing extraordinary," Manners answered. "He's a pro, all right—or he was—but certainly not in your league."

"His name?"

"His prints say he's Henry Johns, but he hasn't used that name for quite a while."

That name, and the name he had found in the man's wallet, meant nothing to Nick. Could this be the man who had been knocking off American couriers for so long?

"You don't look pleased," Manners said. "Did I say something you didn't want to hear?"

"Yes," Nick said, standing up. "But I won't hold it against you. It's not your fault. Thanks for the information . . . and for my gun."

"That's what I'm here for, or so they tell me," Manners said, and now he didn't sound bitter, just weary. "If there's anything else I can do, just let me know."

"I will. Good day."

Manners gave Nick a small salute, and then Nick left and went back to his hotel, much sooner than he had expected.

He decided not to let Stephanie know he was back yet. This would give him time to examine the drawings he'd found at the farmhouse.

He took off his jacket, sat on the bed, and pulled the new drawings out of his inner pocket. There were four of them and he smoothed them out as best he could, then fanned them out on the bed.

They were the same type, with stick-figure men, one killing or trying to kill the other one. One of the drawings plainly gave away Anton Lector's next stop—Rome. One particular drawing showed two stick-figure men standing in front of the Colosseum in Rome, and this bothered Nick. It was as if Lector were leaving signposts, wanting Nick to follow him, but not catch him—yet.

Nick didn't like the feeling of being led around by the nose. He didn't like it at all. He folded up the drawings and put them back in his jacket. He had the papers in one pocket and the five tubes in the other. He laid the jacket across the back of a chair and went into the bathroom to wash his hands. When he came out, Stephanie was standing in the connecting doorway, fully dressed.

She was holding her gun.

TWENTY-FIVE

"I thought I heard you," she said. "You came back earlier than you told me you would."

He was standing in the bathroom doorway with a towel in his hands.

"You can't be that mad," he said, indicating the gun in her hand, "just because I came back earlier than I said."

"What?" she asked, and then looked down at the gun as if she hadn't realized she was holding it. "Oh, this? Don't be silly. I was trying to reload the damned thing when I thought I heard you."

Nick put the towel down and walked up to her.

"Here, let me do it before you shoot yourself in the foot."

He ejected the partially empty clip and inserted the new one she'd been holding.

"I thought it would be better to have it fully loaded," she said as he handed it back.

"It would be better to have it set on safety, too," he said, showing her how to do it.

"Thanks," she said. "Shall I order breakfast?"

"Let's go downstairs and have it," he suggested.

"Let me have a few seconds and I'll be right with you," she said.

"I've heard that before."

She flashed him a mischievous look and walked back into

her own room, leaving the door open.

Nick retrieved his jacket and slipped into it. He knew he should take the time to clean Wilhelmina, just to make sure she was right, but if the killer was dead, then the immediate danger was over.

But how could the killer have been such an unremarkable man? At least he had expected the identification to be someone he had heard of, with a long record of impressive kills.

Nothing had been right about this assignment since the beginning, and it looked as if things would keep right on going that way.

TWENTY-SIX

When Nick told Stephanie where the trail was leading them next, she put her fork down and stared at him.

"Rome?"

"Yes," he said. "One of the drawings I picked up at the farmhouse made it plain." He showed her the drawing in question.

"What if it's wrong?"

"A drawing led us here, didn't it?" he reminded her.

"You needed an imagination to make that one work," she said. "If this one is so obvious . . ." She stared pointedly at the drawing.

"Then it might be a ruse? I thought of that, but we've got no other choice right now, Stephanie. We can't hang around here. Sooner or later that superintendent is going to want to have another chat with me, especially when Belnap is discovered."

"All right, Nick," she said, "you're the boss."

"I'll remind you that you said that sometime."

"Said what?"

"Eat your breakfast."

After breakfast they went back upstairs so they could pack. Since Nick hadn't unpacked, all he had to do was call the airlines and get a flight to their next destination.

Nick stopped by Stephanie's door and waited until she

went in. Then he let himself into his own room and found out that he had company.

"Ah, Mr. . . . French, isn't it?" Superintendent Rheiner said. "Come in, come in. After all, this is your room."

"That's right, it is," Nick said. He closed the door behind him and then faced Rheiner and the two uniformed men he had brought with him. "What's this about, Superintendent?"

"It's about murder," Rheiner answered. "Two murders, in fact. You'd be surprised to know that we don't have that many murders in my city—that is, we didn't until you came. That bothers me. You see, I do not believe in coincidence."

"Well, that makes two of us," Nick said. He had the feeling that things were not going to go well here, and he had to do something before things went totally wrong. "I don't believe in coincidence, either," he said, walking to the chest of drawers on his right. He started emptying his pockets as if he did that every time he came into the room. Wallet, keys, change, and then, hoping that it didn't look too out of place, he took the silver tubes from his pocket and put them in the top drawer, keeping up a line of chatter the whole time to distract the superintendent from what he was doing.

"Excuse me," Rheiner said suddenly, "but I did not come here to discuss coincidence."

"No, I didn't think so," Nick said. He turned to face the man again and rested his elbow on the chest of drawers. "Just what is it you did come here for?"

"To arrest you."

Nick rubbed his jaw with his right hand and then said, "To arrest me . . . for what?"

"I will think of something," Rheiner said.

Nick laughed, which made the superintendent frown.

"What are you laughing at?"

"You," Nick said. "You sound like an American movie."

"I am sorry you find me funny, Mr. French—or whatever your name is—but I do not like CIA men coming into my city and killing people. Do you understand?"

"Understand what?" Nick asked. "You think I'm with the CIA?" Nick gave the superintendent the benefit of his best derisive snort and said, "You've got it all wrong, Rheiner."

"I see. You are merely a tourist here on holiday. . . ."

"Right."

"And the American consulate makes it a point to recover all of their tourists' guns for them, eh?"

The man had him there. How could he explain that away and keep himself out of jail?

He couldn't.

"I think perhaps you should come with us willingly," Rheiner said.

"I've got a right to make a phone call," Nick said, storming past Rheiner and his men and picking up the phone. He started dialing, but Rheiner stopped him by taking the receiver from his hand and putting it down on the table.

"You will be allowed to make your phone call, Mr. French—later!"

"This isn't right, Rheiner," Nick said. "You've got no evidence to arrest me with."

"Mr. French," Rheiner said, "this is not the United States. Please do not presume to tell me what I can and cannot do. Now, I would prefer that you come with us willingly, but if not, we are prepared—"

"Whoa, hold on!" Nick cried, holding his hands up in front of him as the two uniformed policemen approached him. "I'll come willingly, don't worry. I'm sure this is all just a mix-up. CIA man . . ."

As he started past Rheiner, the man put his hand on his chest to stop him and said, "Your weapon, please."

"Oh, yeah, sure," Nick said. He took Wilhelmina out of her holster and handed the gun over. "Uh, before we go, do you mind if I go to the bathroom?"

Rheiner looked annoyed, but agreed.

"Happens when I get nervous," Nick said as he walked to the bathroom and shut the door behind him.

The first time he'd been taken to the police station, they had put him in a room and given him a rather cursory pat-down, but he figured that this time he'd get a pretty thorough body search, and Hugo and Pierre would be, if anything, even harder to explain than Wilhelmina. He took off the knife and the little gas bomb and tucked them away in the medicine chest, then flushed the toilet, washed his hands, and went back into the other room.

"All right, I'm ready."

"If you don't mind . . ." Rheiner said, and then motioned to his men, who approached Nick and patted him down. They stepped back and shook their heads.

"Don't tell me; let me guess," Nick said. "You thought I had a gun hidden in the toilet."

"The thought crossed my mind," Rheiner admitted. "Shall we go?"

Shaking his head, Nick said, "You've really got to stop watching those American movies, Superintendent."

"It may be quite a long time before you get to see any kind of a movie, Mr. French," the man said. "If I were you, I would think about that."

TWENTY-SEVEN

This time they didn't just put Nick in a room, they gave him a cell all his own. Then they gave him a thorough body search, removed his belt and shoelaces, and put him in a cell in the basement of the building.

"I will be by a little later on, Mr. French," Rheiner told him. "Meanwhile, make yourself as comfortable as possible."

"You're making a mistake, Superintendent," Nick said.

"That remains to be seen."

This was a rare situation for Nick. Normally, he was able to use certain connections to keep himself out of jail—not that he made a habit of breaking the law while he was on assignment, but on occasion it had been necessary to bend it a little.

He sat on his cot, and remembered that he had been dialing Stephanie's room when the superintendent grabbed the phone away from him. He hoped she had answered the phone and had listened to the conversation. If she had, there was a chance she'd get in touch with Manners and have him get Nick out of this before they got too far behind Dr. Lector to ever find him.

Nick made good use of the time that he was to spend in that cell. Rather than lament his present situation, he made the best of it by using the time to think, to try and put things together.

He still did not know what Stephanie's whole story was, how she had been able to follow him to London and Paris, but he knew that he was somehow being led around by someone, not necessarily by Lector himself, but by someone who knew Lector's moves and wanted to keep Nick on his trail.

And then there was the killer, who was always one step in front of Nick—but was now dead himself.

Or was he?

Nick was starting to believe that either the dead man wasn't the courier killer, or else there were two men working together, and now one was dead and the other was still out there.

If that was true, then the other man was still a very big threat to all of them—Stephanie, Lector, and himself.

Which brought everything back to his getting out of the predicament he was in. Who knew what the killer would do now that he was out of his reach?

There wasn't very much Nick could do about it at the moment, though. It all rested in the hands of the others: Stephanie, Rheiner, and Manners. He only hoped that the three of them would be able to get it done—and quickly.

He couldn't tell for sure, because they had taken his watch as well, but it must have been five or six hours before Rheiner came back and opened the cell door.

"Come with me," he said, looking unhappy.

"Am I sprung?"

"Just follow me, Mr. French, and don't try my patience," the smaller man said. "I am on edge at this moment, and what I do not need is a push from you."

"All right, Superintendent," Nick said, standing up, "lead the way."

Rheiner led him upstairs and into the room where they had first taken him. Waiting for them there was David Manners. On the table in the center of the room were Nick's watch, belt, shoelaces, and gun.

"Here is your man, Mr. Manners," Rheiner said. "Remember your promise, please." With that, the superintendent left without casting another glance at Nick.

"Are you all right?" Manners asked Nick.

"Yes, I am," Nick said, collecting his things from the table. "What was that about?"

"Let's get out of here and then we'll talk," Manners said.

"I'm for that."

Manners had a car waiting for them outside, and in the back seat was Stephanie.

"Are you all right?" she asked when they entered the car.

"I'm fine."

"I got so scared when you called my room," she said. "I almost hung up, but then I heard you and the policeman talking, and I saw them take you away. All I could think to do was call the consulate."

"You did just right," Nick told her. He turned to Manners and asked, "What about this promise you made to Rheiner?"

"I promised him the murderer of Kaufman and the farmer, Belnap, and I promised him that you would leave the city and the country immediately."

"Well, that fits right in with my plans," Nick said. "We were about to leave when I was arrested."

"Then I suggest you do so."

"You don't want me here any more than Rheiner does," Nick said. "So how about having your car wait for us at the hotel while we pack and settle up?"

"That's fine with me. I'll have the driver drop me off first, and then he'll take you to the airport."

They dropped Manners off, and he left the car without a word to either of them. Stephanie turned to Nick and said, "And where are we off to now, as if I didn't know?"

"The next stop," Nick said, "is Rome."

TWENTY-EIGHT

During the flight from Geneva to Rome, Nick made a decision on how they would proceed.

They wouldn't.

He decided to take that feeling—which came from instinct—that someone was leading him about, and run with it. He was not even going to make an attempt at finding Anton Lector and, if he was right, something would happen to tell him where to look next.

He was hoping that this course of action might also answer some questions about Stephanie. Maybe she would be the one to come up with something on Lector, which would be immediately questionable. She wasn't supposed to be interested in anything but finding her father's killer. If all of a sudden she was able to come up with something helpful on Dr. Lector, that would mean that she wasn't what she seemed to be.

Then he would have to find out who she really was, and who was directing her.

He looked at Stephanie, dozing in the seat next to him, and wondered if he'd ever really know what her real goal was.

When their descent was announced, Nick nudged Stephanie and they fastened their seat belts.

"I was asleep," she said.

"I noticed," he told her, smiling. She smiled back, and her smile made her incredibly lovely. He hoped that she was no more than what she seemed, a lovely young woman who was deeply affected by the death—no, the murder—of a father she had loved very much.

"Have you been making plans?" she said.

"Oh, yes," he said. "Very definite plans."

Definite plans to do nothing but wait and see what happened.

TWENTY-NINE

At the hotel, Nick surprised Stephanie by asking for a single suite, but she kept quiet. When they got into the room and the bellboy left, she sidled up to Nick and put her arms around his waist.

"I get the feeling you want something of me this trip, sir," she said, kissing his throat.

He closed his arms around her and when she tilted her head up, he kissed her, softly at first, and then harder, until she broke away, panting slightly. She put one hand between them and felt his hardness.

"You do want something, don't you?"

They moved together toward the bed, then separated long enough to undress and pull down the covers. After that, they were on the bed, rolling in each other's arms, and when he entered her, she stiffened and raked his back with her nails.

He proceeded slowly at first as he teased her with his mouth and tongue, kissing her gently all over her face, then her neck, until he finally found her breasts. When he felt the urgency of her body beneath him, he sped up to match her thrusts. He could feel her body stiffening and knew she was ready. He increased his momentum and felt her body lift from the bed just as his own world exploded before him. They were together physically, yet lost for the moment in their own separate bliss.

"Oh yes," she said when their spasms had subsided and they were lying together on the bed. She stretched, and he watched as her lithe, young body went taut, her breasts flattening on her chest. And then she laid one hand on his belly and began to make circles.

"It's too bad," she said.

"What is?"

"It's too bad we didn't just meet by accident in Washington and find each other. It's too bad that this isn't all that we have between us," she said, playing with the hair on his chest.

"Stephanie—" he started to say.

"I'm getting too serious, huh?" she jumped in. "Don't worry, Nick, I don't expect anything from you after all this is over. All I ever expected from you was to find my father's killer."

"I never promised—"

"I know, I know," she assured him. "Don't worry about it." She leaned over, and flattening her breasts on his chest, kissed his mouth lightly. "I'm going to take a shower."

He watched her as she got up off the bed and walked to the bathroom, enjoying the way the muscles in her sleek buttocks clenched and unclenched as she walked. When she closed the door behind her, he sat up and swung his feet to the floor. Out of the corner of his eye he spotted the phone and, on impulse, picked it up.

"Desk."

"This is Mr. Genova in room nine-fourteen."

"Yes, sir," the clerk said in careful, precise English.

"I would like a car and a driver in front of the hotel at seven-thirty to take myself and a guest to the finest restaurant in the area."

"Of course, sir."

"Will you make a reservation for two, please?"

"It would be our pleasure," the clerk said.

"Thank you."

"You are quite welcome, sir."

Nick checked his watch and saw that they had almost three hours before it would be time to go downstairs and meet the car. He heard the shower running behind the bathroom door. He had intended to take a shower anyway, so why wait?

He opened the bathroom door and stepped into the steamy room. There were not only rivulets of water running down the mirror, but down the walls as well.

Stephanie heard him and called out, "Hey, what's the matter? Can't you wait your turn?"

He pulled aside the shower curtain and Stephanie looked at him, holding the soap in front of her with both hands.

Water and soap suds were running down her body. Her breasts gleamed as if they were made of marble.

"I thought we were supposed to be partners," he said. "Don't you want to share your shower with me?"

"Why not?" she asked. "I've shared everything else with you, haven't I?" She extended her hand to him, holding the soap, and said, "Why not my soap?"

THIRTY

Stephanie was very curious when, at seven o'clock, Nick told her to get dressed, they were going out.

"Where?"

"You'll see," he said. "I've got a car that will be waiting for us in front of the hotel in a half an hour."

"Half an hour," she cried, leaping off the bed, where they had spent the better part of two hours after they had gotten out of the shower. "You don't give a girl much time to get ready."

"You look fine," he said. "Just throw something on."

"Sure," she said, running to the bathroom, "throw something on, the man says!"

He heard the shower start running again, and he was sure she would be at least an hour getting ready. But she surprised him by being ready when he was, and they went downstairs.

There was a large, black limo waiting for them in front of the hotel, with a uniformed driver leaning against it. When he saw them, he straightened up and opened the back door.

"I'm impressed," Stephanie said. "When did you have time to do this?"

"I made time."

They got into the car and the driver walked around it, got behind the wheel, and started off.

"You're being very mysterious about this," she said.

"Does it have something to do with—"

"You'll see what it has to do with," he said. He took her hand, and from the corner of his eye saw that this surprised her—as everything he had done since they arrived in Rome had been surprising her.

They drove for about twenty minutes, and then the driver stopped the car in front of a well-lit, busy restaurant.

"Here?" she said, looking the place over through the window.

"You want to eat, don't you?"

"Is that all we're doing, going out to dinner?" she asked.

"What did you expect?"

She stared at him speechlessly for a few moments and then shook her head and said, "I don't know."

"Well, come on, then," he said. The driver had opened the door, and Nick stepped out and then reached in to help Stephanie.

Nick told the driver he could go, but he was to come back for them in about an hour and a half.

"An hour and a half?" Stephanie repeated. "We'll be lucky to get a table in an hour."

"I've made reservations," he assured her.

"You're full of surprises, aren't you?"

"Let's go before they give our table away," he said, taking her by the elbow.

When they got inside, the maître d' asked if he could be of assistance, first in Italian, and then in English.

"We have a reservation," Nick said. "Mr. and Mrs. Genova."

He was aware of Stephanie's short intake of breath, but ignored it and ushered her ahead of him as they were shown to their table.

"A drink?" he asked her.

"Red wine," she said. He told the waiter to bring her a red wine and a bourbon for him.

When the waiter left, she said, "I didn't see you sign in this afternoon. Mr. and Mrs.?"

"Do you object?"

"I'm just surprised, that's all," she said, but he could see that her surprise was rapidly turning into puzzlement.

During dinner, he didn't talk about his assignment once. Instead, he asked her about herself and what she planned to do when she got back home. He asked her about her childhood, her parents, anything but what had been happening to them the past week.

"Nick?" she asked over dessert.

"Yes?"

"What are you planning to do?"

"Now?" he asked. "Why, enjoy the dessert, and the delightful company."

"No, I mean about your assignment."

"My assignment," he repeated. "I don't even want to think about that now. Did you know that you're very beautiful?"

She frowned and said, "That's very nice to hear, Nick, but don't you think you should be thinking about—"

"Coffee," he said.

"What?"

"More coffee," he said, signaling the waiter.

"Nick—"

"Stephanie, I don't want to talk about business tonight," he said, cutting her off. "In fact, I think I'll have some bourbon in that coffee."

As he turned to look for the waiter again, he could actually feel her eyes on him, puzzling, wondering what was wrong.

Actually, he was enjoying himself. During the last few hours with her, he had relaxed—not totally, but to a certain degree. And she certainly was an enthusiastic bed partner.

But what else was she?

THIRTY-ONE

When they got back to the hotel, Nick carried on the drunk act that he had started in the restaurant. Stephanie had had to go outside and ask the driver to come in and help bring Nick to the car. Now she had a bellboy help her get him up to the room, and then tipped him generously.

"Nick, I don't know what's gotten into you," she said. She and the bellboy had dumped him on the bed, and now she began to undress him. As her hands tugged at his pants and came into contact with his flesh, there was a reaction that was unavoidable. Surely, a truly drunken man would not have reacted in the same way—would he?—but he hoped that the question would not enter her mind, as well.

"You are a beautiful man, Nick," she said after she had taken off his pants and shirt. "Even when you're drunk." Her hand plucked at the waistband of his shorts, as if she were trying to make up her mind. "Very hard to resist," she was saying, and then she took hold of the waistband and pulled the shorts down to his ankles, and off.

He felt her hands on his erection then, and moaned for effect. Her hands disappeared and he dared not open his eyes to see what she was doing, but the rustle of her clothing on her flesh told him that she was undressing.

"You're in my power," she whispered, and then he heard her giggle and felt his penis slide between her breasts. He moaned again, and this time it was half for effect and half involuntary. Then suddenly he felt the warmth of her mouth claim him and he gave in entirely.

He was very glad he had decided to leave Hugo and Pierre behind when they went to dinner. She had removed his shoulder holster along with the rest of his clothes, but he didn't want her to have to fiddle with Pierre. The last thing he needed was for her to set the little gas bomb off by accident.

"Nick," she said, and suddenly her mouth was too busy for her to speak. He could hold back no longer and groaned out loud as he climaxed.

When she freed his penis, he heard her say, "Oh, Nick, even half asleep . . ." and she ran her hands over his belly and chest. "Sleep," she whispered in his ear. "Sleep, darling."

He felt her rise from the bed and heard her walk away. He chanced opening his eyes and saw her putting on her robe. After that, she went into the bathroom and closed the door behind her. He wished she had at least put his shorts back on, because he was starting to feel a draft.

She was in the bathroom for about twenty minutes, and when the door opened, he closed his eyes again. When she came out, he was lying in exactly the same position.

"Still asleep, Nick?" he heard her call out. Then, "Yup, he's still asleep. Too bad."

He felt her walk past his feet, then felt her again as she sat down at the head of the bed.

Right by the phone!

He risked opening his eyes and saw her sitting with her back to him, apparently studying the phone. She's wondering whether she should make a call or not, he thought. He continued to watch her back, and then she shrugged and reached for the phone.

She told the operator she wanted to call the United States, and gave a number. Apparently the operator asked if she wanted to call person-to-person, because she said, "That's all right, operator. There should only be one person there to answer it."

There was a short silence. She turned once to look at him, and then she started talking.

"Yes, it's me," she said into the phone, and he opened his eyes again.

"No, it's not going right," she said. "It went wrong in Geneva, and he's been acting funny since we got to Rome."

She listened a few seconds and then said, "Right now he's passed out on the . . . on his bed. He took me to dinner, drank too much, and never once mentioned his assignment." Silence, and then, "I know it's not like him. I'm worried. . . . Of course I'm not getting involved. . . . Well, you better do something. He doesn't seem at all interested in finishing this thing. . . . No, I don't know what he's interested in. . . . yes, I'll stay with him. I've got to get off now. I'll keep in touch. Good-bye."

She hung up, and he closed his eyes because he knew she would automatically turn around and look to see if he was listening. She had taken a big chance making that call from his room, but he must have totally confused her and she had needed guidance immediately.

But whose?

He finally allowed her to rouse him sufficiently to maneuver him underneath the covers with her, whereupon she draped a silky thigh and a warm arm over him and went to sleep.

Sleep eluded Nick. The phone call was bothering him. He wished he'd been able to hear something of the conversation from the other end. He didn't even know whether she had been talking to a man or a woman—although it seemed unlikely that it would have been a woman.

He put one arm around Stephanie's waist and she snuggled in closer, moaning a bit in her sleep. He was sorry she had turned out to be more than she seemed, but he wasn't going to let it keep him awake any longer.

The next move was either hers or whoever she had spoken to on the phone, and he doubted they would waste much time. He wanted to be well-rested come morning, and he had to make sure he remembered that he had been drunk the night before.

Stephanie had come to bed totally naked, and now she was rubbing up against him in her sleep, eliciting the natural response from Nick.

You're in a drunken stupor, he told himself, but there was a certain part of his body that refused to be convinced and which didn't care what she was beyond the fact that she was a lovely female and close by.

It took all of Nick's willpower for him to turn over so that they were cheek to cheek. When he was comfortable, he forced himself to go to sleep.

THIRTY-TWO

The next morning Nick made all of the appropriate noises, and Stephanie recommended that he take a shower. She gave him five minutes alone in the bathroom, and then joined him.

"You seem much better now," she said as she stepped into the shower with him and ran her hands over his body.

"I'm feeling better, all right," he said, returning the favor, "but not as good as you feel."

They splashed around until they were both satisfied, then cleaned each other off and stepped out.

"I'll dry you first," she said.

"Let's dry ourselves, or we're liable to get all involved again," he suggested.

She smiled and said, "All right."

"I'm sorry about last night," he said.

"You deserved it, I guess," she replied.

"I did?"

"Well, after being in jail and all, I guess you just wanted to relax."

She was handing him an excuse on a silver platter, so he decided to take it.

"You might be right," he agreed.

"Anyway, I enjoyed myself."

"I'm glad."

"Especially after we got back," she added with a sly look.

He stopped short with one leg in his pants and one leg out and said, "Did I miss something?"

"Oh, I think you enjoyed it—or maybe you thought it was a wet dream."

"I haven't had a wet dream in—oh, weeks now," Nick said, finishing with his pants and putting on a shirt.

"What shall we do today?" she asked, dropping her towel and bending over her suitcase to find something to wear.

Eyeing her smooth buttocks, he said, "I just got an urge to go sight-seeing."

She looked over her shoulder at him and grinned, then started getting dressed.

"Why don't we have breakfast and then go for a walk?" he suggested. "Maybe something will come up."

"All right," she agreed.

He finished dressing and said, "I'll go down to the hotel dining room and get us a table. I'll meet you down there in—"

"About a half an hour," she finished. "A girl's got to look right."

"I've heard that," he said. "Ciao."

He left the room and wondered if she was making another phone call. Probably not. One was chancy enough, and everything appeared to have been said. He wondered when he would see the result of that call, and in what form it would come.

He grabbed a table in the dining room and ordered a pot of coffee to work on while he waited for her.

He had ordered a second pot by the time she finally showed up, and he smiled at her as she sat down. He said, "It was worth the wait—again."

She touched his hand and said, "You're so understanding."

"That's me," he said. "Want a menu?"

"No," she said. "I'll take the continental breakfast. Might as well stick with a good thing."

"Right."

Nick called the waiter over and ordered the same thing for both of them.

"You got a call while I was dressing," she said after he had ordered.

"I did?" he asked. "From whom?"

"A man. He wouldn't tell me who he was, but he gave me a number to give you and asked that you call him back as soon as possible."

"Do you remember the number?"

"I have it written down," she said, opening her purse.

"Wait," he said as he spotted the waiter returning with their juice.

She continued rummaging through her purse while the waiter put down their juice and promised that their breakfasts would be along very shortly.

"Thank you," Nick said. The man executed a short bow, cast an admiring glance Stephanie's way, and then left.

"Here's the phone number," she said, handing him a slip of paper.

He read the number, then folded it and put it away in his pocket.

"Is it important?" she asked, contriving to look innocent.

"It could be," he said, noncommittally. "It could very well be."

Actually, it was all getting out of hand now, because the number on the slip of paper was a number that Stephanie Clark—DIA employee or not—should have never had.

It was a direct "safe" line to David Hawk.

THIRTY-THREE

After breakfast, Nick suggested that Stephanie stay in the dining room and wait for him while he went up to the room.

"Are you going to return that call?"

"Yes," he said, standing up. "I'll be back in a little while. Have some more coffee."

She nodded and he left the dining room and went up to his room. He debated using the phone or converting the hotel television with the equipment from his suitcase's false bottom. He opted for the television set and in a short time was looking at the face of David Hawk.

"Well, N3," Hawk said, "I was beginning to get curious. I assume you've been busy."

"Yes, sir," Nick said. He reported to his superior everything that had occurred since they'd last spoken, but he made no mention of the fact that Stephanie claimed he'd received a phone message to call Hawk's private number.

"You *have* been busy," Hawk said when Nick's report was finished. "I suppose you would like me to check on likely people Dr. Lector might want to see in Rome?"

"Yes, sir," Nick said. "That would be a help."

"Hopefully they will be alive when you arrive," Hawk said. "Do you believe that the man in the barn was our killer?"

"I have my doubts, sir."

"Oh? What indication have you had otherwise?"

"None, sir."

Hawk looked bored and said, "Instinct?"

"Yes, sir."

"I can't very well argue with that, N3," Hawk said. "We'll just have to wait and see if you are right. I presume you are maintaining your level of caution."

"Yes, sir."

"Is Miss Clark still with you?"

"Yes, she is."

"Has she been a hindrance?"

"No, sir. As I outlined, it was she who was instrumental in getting me out of jail in Geneva."

"Of course. Is the, uh, 'round peg' safe?"

If it wasn't, I would have told you right off, Nick thought, but he nodded and told his boss, "Yes, sir, quite safe."

"Very good. All right, N3. Try and keep in more frequent contact from here on in. This 'round peg' you are carrying is quite important to us, and to other countries as well, if they were to get their hands on it."

"I'm fully aware of that, sir."

"Good," Hawk said, and broke contact.

Nick dismantled the communications device thoughtfully. Not one mention of a phone call, and Hawk had asked if Miss Clark was still with him. If he had spoken to her that morning, he would have known without asking.

Stephanie had lied, but where had she gotten that phone number—through the DIA computer?

By all rights, he should have mentioned to Hawk the fact that his number was no longer private, but he'd held off and would later plead that it had been a decision made, again, by instinct.

He put his equipment back into the false bottom of his suitcase, closed and locked it. He walked to the window and looked down at the street in front of the hotel. Stephanie knew she was lying, so how would she react when he made no mention of it? And why would she lie so blatantly, knowing that he'd find out almost immediately.

There was only one answer to that question, and he left his position by the window and looked around the room very quickly. Her suitcase was gone, and her clothing had not been unpacked. He hurried down to the dining room, knowing now that he was right. As he expected, she was not there waiting for him.

He went to the desk next.

"Excuse me."

The clerk looked up and said, "Yes?"

"I'm Mr. Genova, room nine-fourteen."

"Yes, sir. How may we serve you?"

"Can you tell me if my wife checked out?"

"Your . . . wife, sir?" the clerk asked, looking puzzled.

"I know it sounds strange, but could you check, please?"

"Of course, sir, right away," the clerk said, looking at Nick strangely. The man could not be Italian, he thought, losing his own wife.

And then he found it.

"Yes, Mr. Genova," the man said, bringing the registration card over for Nick to look at. "She checked out only moments ago."

"I see," Nick said, glancing at the card. "If she had checked her bag prior to that, where would she have done so?"

"There," the clerk said, pointing to a window to his right.

"Thank you," Nick said, and walked over to the man standing behind the window. Remembering that he *was* in Italy, he decided that the best way for the man to remember Stephanie was to describe her. No Italian man could forget her once he had seen her.

"Oh, si, signor," the man said, "she was here only minutes ago. Your wife, signor, she is—how do you say it in English—very lovely."

''Yes, thank you,'' Nick said. ''Did you see where she went?''

''Regretfully, no, signor,'' the man said. ''But perhaps the doorman can help you.''

''Undoubtedly,'' Nick said. ''Thank you again.'' He tipped the man generously and went outside to talk to the doorman.

''Si, signor,'' the doorman said, fondling the money Nick had given him. ''Your wife, she got into a taxi.''

''Did you hear her tell the driver where she wanted to go?''

''I am sorry, signor, no. I was called away. . . .''

''That's all right,'' Nick told him. ''Thank you.''

He went back into the hotel to the bar and ordered a bourbon. He thought about the developments of the morning. First she told him a blatant lie, and all the while she had intended to leave afterward. That was why she had taken extra time in the room, to pack, and then to check her bags before meeting him in the dining room.

Now she was gone, but where, and to do what? Nick decided that he would contact Hawk again that evening, and when he did, he would ask him to check further into Stephanie Clark's background. An identification card was easy to forge, and perhaps he had accepted her too readily in the beginning as his dead friend's daughter.

He was convinced that the courier killer was still out there somewhere, and who said it had to be a man?

THIRTY-FOUR

Nick was at loose ends for the remainder of the day. As far as his assignment was concerned, he was helpless to take any action without further information. He decided to try and find the cab that had picked up Stephanie that morning and then find out where it had taken her.

In theory, this was simple detective legwork, since the same fleet of cabs serviced the hotel, but with the number of cabs, it still took a good portion of the day to find the right driver.

Several times he had been asked for a photograph of his "wife," but he had to be satisfied with simply describing her to the men who, being Italian, immediately wished they *had* picked her up.

Except for the last one. He recognized Stephanie's description right away.

"Beautiful," the man said, drawing the word out as if very proud of his English.

"Do you remember where you took her?"

"Of course, signor."

"Good, take me there."

"Your wife, eh?" the man said, starting the car. Obviously he assumed that Stephanie was a cheating wife who was about to be found by her cuckolded husband. "I will take you there, signor. Have no fear."

Nick half-expected the man to take him to the airport, but it soon became obvious that he was not. They drove for about a half an hour and then pulled up in front of a small hotel.

"Here, signor," the man said, turning around with a wide grin.

"Here?"

"Right there," the driver said, pointing. "I stayed to, eh, watch her—" the man said, stopping to give a "who wouldn't?" shrug, "—and she went right into that hotel."

"All right," Nick said. He paid the fare and tipped the man. As he got out of the car, the driver called out to him.

"I hope you catch her, signor!"

Nick waved and walked toward the hotel, then veered off. Across the street, he spotted a small cafe with outdoor tables and decided to have a cup of coffee and wait a while. He still had a few hours to kill.

Settled at the table with a cup of brandy-laced coffee, he wished he could take a chance and walk into the lobby, but there was always the possibility that she would be coming out of an elevator or the dining room and spot him. He didn't want to spook her. He knew where she was—hopefully—and that was good enough for now. He would sit there for a few hours and hope to spot her coming out. No woman could stay in a hotel room in Italy for very long without having to come out for air. If she didn't come out tonight, he'd go back to his own hotel and contact Hawk for the information he needed. Finding Dr. Lector was still top priority, but if Stephanie Clark turned out to be an imposter, he could come back for her.

After waiting a couple of hours, Nick was about to give it up when the front door of the hotel opened and out walked Stephanie. He sat back down and watched her as she made her way down the street at a leisurely pace. She wasn't carrying any luggage, so presumably she was just going for a walk, or for dinner, but there was no longer any doubt that she was staying at that hotel.

He waited until she had walked out of sight, then caught a taxi and took it back to his hotel.

It was time to get in touch with Hawk again—and get back to work.

THIRTY-FIVE

"When I said to keep in touch more frequently, N3, I didn't expect you to take me so literally," Hawk said when Nick established contact.

"There have been other developments," Nick said.

"Oh? Such as?"

Nick told Hawk that Stephanie Clark had checked herself out of the hotel and disappeared.

"She wasn't forced?" Hawk asked.

"No, not according to my information."

"Well, then, if she's left of her own free will, she must have given up her thirst for revenge," Hawk suggested. "Unless she believes that the man you killed in Geneva was her father's killer, in which case she's satisfied. Either way, she is out of your hair now."

"That's one way of looking at it," Nick said. "In any case, I'd like to check into her background. I want to be sure that this girl is who she says she is."

"I checked into her background when you first mentioned her to me, N3," Hawk said patiently. "The girl appears to be genuine."

"Appears to be?"

Hawk was beginning to get impatient now.

"A poor choice of words on my part," he said. "The girl is who she says she is. Now, I have that other information for you, the names of the people to whom Dr. Lector might go for help."

"All right," Nick said, and he listened while Hawk rattled off three names and addresses, which he then wrote down. Three more innocent people . . .

"Now you can forget about Stephanie Clark and get to the business at hand," Hawk finished.

"That's right," Nick agreed.

"I would tell you to stay in touch, but I'm afraid you would be calling me in a few hours."

"I'll get in touch when I've checked out these three people."

"Do you feel like you're getting closer to finding the good doctor?" Hawk asked, uncharacteristically. It was the kind of question someone would ask just to keep a conversation going. Hawk had never had that problem—or inclination—before.

"No, sir, I don't," Nick answered honestly. "I don't feel any closer than I did the day I left your office."

"That's not very encouraging."

Nick frowned and said, "You don't usually want encouraging news if there isn't any."

A shadow passed over Hawk's face and he said, "Of course not," and broke contact.

The old man was acting strange, Nick thought as he dismantled the TV device. In fact, everything about this case was strange, and getting stranger by the second.

Nick was starting to feel very alone on this, as if he had been hung out to dry—and he didn't like the feeling at all.

He checked the list of names and addresses given to him by Hawk and figured he'd have to put himself in the hands of some cab driver who knew the city well.

Nick still had the drawings he had found, supposedly drawn by Anton Lector, and was now wondering if he would find more of them at one of the locations.

More and more, it seemed to him that someone was leaving him the drawings, like a roadmap . . . but to where?

THIRTY-SIX

He grabbed a taxi in front of the hotel and gave the driver the first address, mispronouncing the street name. The driver shook his head, corrected him, and then started off.

The address turned out to be an apartment building, a far cry from what the places had looked like in Paris and Geneva. Lector seemed to have a higher class of friends in Rome.

Nick went inside and was approached by a uniformed doorman.

"Can I help you, sir?" the man asked in English, which puzzled Nick a bit. How had the man known that he spoke English and not Italian—or even Swahili? Why English?

"I'd like to see Antonio Bellomo, please."

"A moment," the doorman said. He walked to a small desk where he picked up a phone, dialed a few numbers, spoke shortly, then nodded. He hung up and approached Nick.

"You can go up, sir," the man informed him. "Room eleven-thirty."

"Thank you."

The man keyed the elevator for him and when the doors closed, Nick could see the cab sitting out front, waiting for him to come back down.

When the elevator got to the eleventh floor and the doors opened, Nick didn't step out right away. He waited, then took out Wilhelmina and sprang into the hall in a crouch.

He was alone.

Feeling a little foolish—but still unable to shake the feeling that had made him draw his gun in the first place—he put his gun away and started down the hall to room eleven-thirty. He rang the bell, and when there was no answer, tried the knob. It turned easily and he pushed the door open. Drawing his gun again, he stepped carefully into the room.

The drapes at the window were drawn and the room was in semidarkness. The living room was modernly and expensively furnished and amazingly clean, as if it were a model. He went through the rest of the apartment—a kitchen and two bedrooms—and found the same Spartan conditions.

Except for the trash bucket in one of the bedrooms. There were several pieces of crumpled paper in it, and Nick knew what he would find when he picked them up. There were three of them, and when he smoothed them out on a dresser top, he found that here were three more drawings to add to his collection. One of them made it very plain what his next move would be. It showed two stick figures in front of the Washington Monument.

He folded the drawings lengthwise and tucked them into his jacket pocket, still holding his gun in his right hand. It wasn't until he left the apartment that he put the gun away.

In the elevator, he wondered if he should follow the direction dictated by the drawing, or go to the other two addresses first to check them out, also.

When the elevator doors opened on the main floor, the first thing he noticed was the absence of the uniformed doorman. He looked behind the desk and saw that, wherever the man had gone, he had left his hat behind.

As he walked toward the front doors, he looked out and noticed the second thing that was out of whack.

His cab was gone.

He had instructed the man to wait and had paid him extra

money to do so with the promise of more. No cabbie, no matter what country he was in, would give up the promise of a big fare.

Unless he was forced to.

Nick put his hand on the door, but didn't push it open. He peered through the glass and looked up and down the block as far as he could see, then examined the buildings across the street. There could have been a man with a rifle in any of the windows, just waiting for him to come out.

Suddenly, as if to prove that point, he heard a crunching sound, and a bullet punched a clean hole in the glass just to his left and level with his head. The slug imbedded itself in the wall behind him. Nick ducked behind the only cover he had in the small entry foyer, the doorman's desk. He didn't pull his gun out, because he had nothing to shoot at.

Another bullet came through the glass, only not too cleanly this time. The entire top portion of the glass door starred, and then a third bullet came through and shattered it into countless pieces.

The rifleman continued to bombard the foyer with bullets, but did not get nearly as many ricochets as he might have hoped for, and none of the ones he did get came anywhere near Nick.

When the firing finally ceased, Nick stuck his head up above the desk and looked across the street again, but he couldn't pick out the window the man was firing from.

There wasn't a shard of glass left in the door, but even though Nick could have run out of the foyer without having to stop to open the door, he knew he would be cut down before he got ten feet. There was no cover in front of the apartment, and he'd be out in the open for much too long. He only had one way out, and that was the elevator. Once he made it to another floor, he could look for another way out of the building.

It was about six feet to the elevator from the desk he was

hiding behind, but the door to the elevator was closed. He would need the key to open it, and he searched behind the desk until he found it. He took a moment to wonder why the doorman—or the man posing as the doorman—had not taken it with him.

Now that he had the key, he would have to run to the door, insert the key in the control panel, and open the elevator door without getting shot. He'd be out in the open for a matter of seconds, but that would be plenty of time for the rifleman to squeeze off a few shots.

As he shifted around behind the desk, he felt it move as he leaned against it. Grasping the side of it, he pulled and found that he was able to move it a few inches. The desk was not very large and he was able to brace one hand against each end of it. Holding it that way, he could drag it with him to the elevator door. He would only have to stand up when he reached the control board, revealing the upper portion of his body. A smaller target, and a bigger chance for him to get away with his life.

As soon as he started dragging the desk toward the door, the rifleman opened up again, firing steadily. After a few slugs had struck the front partition of the desk, one bullet hit and went through, tugging at the sleeve of Nick's jacket. By the time he reached the elevator door, portions of the desk front were shredding.

Nick had the key clutched in his right fist, and now he shifted it so that he was holding it ready to insert in the slot. He waited a few moments to see if the firing would stop, and then was rewarded when it did. No doubt the rifleman was sighting in on that desk, waiting for him to stand up so that he could fire a well-placed shot rather than trying to hit Nick at random.

Nick waited as long as he could, and when the silence began to get deafening, he took a deep breath and stood up, telling himself to ignore everything but the slot into which the key fit.

His hand darted forward and the key was swallowed as clean as a whistle. His back muscles were clenched, waiting for the slug to hit as he turned the key causing the elevator door to slide open. As he threw himself through, a bullet entered the elevator to keep him company, and then the door slid shut and he was safe.

He rode the elevator to the third floor because it had already passed the second before he recovered enough to press a button. As it came to a halt, he drew his gun. When the door opened, he repeated the sequence he had performed on eleven with the same results. He was alone in the hall, but this time he kept his gun handy while he looked for a stairway.

He found one stairway, but it was in the front of the building. He didn't want to come out that way on the off chance that the rifleman would be waiting for him. The other two alternatives were that the man had either run across the street to look for Nick in the building, or that he had given up and left. Whatever the shooter had done after Nick entered the elevator, Nick wanted to find a side or a back way out of the building, just to be on the safe side.

Nick walked back the way he had come and saw that the elevator had stayed on the third floor. It was then that he realized he still held the key to operate it. He dropped the key into a sand urn next to the elevator door and pushed it down until it was buried, then went in search of his exit.

He finally found a freight elevator and pressed the down button to see if it would respond. If it didn't, he'd have to keep searching for a stairway, or else hope that the gunman had left and use the front exit after all. As luck would have it, the freight elevator responded and he rode it down to the main floor. There he found three different exits from the building, which meant that the killer, if he was a gambling man, had one chance in three of picking the right door and waiting for Nick to come out so he could finish his job.

Nick touched the silver tubes that were still in his jacket

pocket, made his choice, opened the door, and stepped out.

The door opened onto a sidestreet, and across the street was a park. There were some mothers watching their children play and a few old people sitting on benches feeding birds, but there was no gunman in sight, and no bullets coming his way.

Holstering Wilhelmina before someone could notice, he walked to the corner and peered around the building. There were a couple of police cars parked in front of the apartment building, and in that moment Nick decided not to check out the other two addresses. He was better off getting out of Rome before he had more trouble with the police. He was tired of jails. He'd grab the earliest plane he could and head to where the new drawings indicated Lector was headed.

Washington D.C.

THIRTY-SEVEN

Back at the hotel he packed up and called the desk to tell them to get his bill ready.

Then he thought about Stephanie.

He knew where she was, but should he just leave without confronting her? According to Hawk, she was who she said she was, Howard Clark's daughter, and Clark was his friend. Did he owe it to Howard to get his daughter out of whatever it was she had gotten herself into?

Nick called the airport and made reservations for two in the names of Mr. and Mrs. Howard.

In the lobby, he settled his bill and then went outside and had the doorman flag a cab for him. He stowed his suitcase in the trunk and then gave the driver the address of the hotel Stephanie was staying in.

"Wait for me," he instructed the driver when they pulled up in front of the hotel, and then went inside to the front desk.

"I'm looking for my wife," he told the man, who listened to his sad story and nodded knowingly. Another cheating wife, the clerk thought, and felt that it was his duty to help his fellow man.

After Nick described Stephanie, the clerk's eye brightened and he showed Nick the registration card. Stephanie had registered as Mrs. S. Carter, which showed imagination on her part.

Armed with the room number, Nick took the elevator to the correct floor and knocked on Stephanie's door. When she asked who it was, he told her room service, and she opened the door.

"Nick!" she said in surprise.

"Hello, Stephanie," he said. "Invite me in."

She stared at him with her mouth open, and he stepped in past her. She shut the door and turned to face him, looking uncertain.

"Nick, I—"

"Never mind," he told her. "Get packed, you're checking out."

"What—"

"Don't ask questions, Stephanie. I've got reservations on a plane that leaves in an hour."

"W-where are we going?"

"We're going home—Mrs. Carter."

THIRTY-EIGHT

Nick had come full circle—London, Paris, Geneva, Rome, and now back to Washington. Maybe this was where Lector was headed all along. Maybe he'd presented himself to Hawk and was safe now.

Before he went to see Hawk, Nick had to make sure Stephanie stayed where he put her. From the airport he made a phone call and arranged for a place to leave her. Sandry Triggs worked in AXE's archives section, and she and Nick had an on-again, off-again thing going. He called her and told her that he had something he would appreciate her watching over. She promised to leave work and meet him at her apartment in a half an hour.

"All right," he told Stephanie, "let's go."

"Where?" she asked. He'd left her sitting far enough away from the phone to prevent her from hearing his conversation, but close enough so that he could grab her if she tried to get away.

"We're going to visit a friend of mine," he answered.

"Why are you treating me like a criminal?" she demanded. "We're back in Washington now, so why don't you go home and let me do the same?"

"We may be home, but we're not finished yet, Stephanie," he said, pulling her along. "You've got a lot of explaining to do, and as soon as we get the time, you're going to do it."

"I don't have to explain anything," she said.

"We'll see."

Outside D.C. International, they picked up a cab, dumped the bags into the trunk, and Nick gave the driver Sandry's address.

When they arrived, Nick allowed Stephanie to carry her own bag, preferring not to have both of his hands full.

"Nick, this is ridiculous—"

"I never knew a woman to travel as light as you do, Stephanie," he said, interrupting her, "but then again, I guess that would come in handy for fast checkouts, right?"

"I can explain—"

"And you will," he said, "but later."

At Sandry's door, he rang the bell and the petite beauty opened it, wearing a smile that disappeared when she saw Stephanie.

"Nick," she said.

"Hi, Sandry," he said, kissing her cheek and ushering Stephanie past her.

"Is this what you want me to keep an eye on?" Sandry asked, shutting the door and turning to examine Stephanie, who was doing some examining of her own.

"This is Stephanie Clark," Nick said. "I have some things to do, Sandry, and I need to know that Stephanie will still be here when I get back."

"I see," Sandry said. "I'm a baby-sitter."

"This is silly—" Stephanie started.

"That's right," Nick said. "I'm sure you girls will find a lot to talk about." He turned to Stephanie and said, "Sandry has a black belt in karate, so I wouldn't try leaving until I get back."

She glared at him and he chucked her under the chin and said, "Cheer up. I'll bring you some french fries."

"You know what you can do with your french fries," she

said, and turned her back on him.

Sandry walked him to the door and said, "Thanks for the promotion."

"Well, you'd like to be a black belt in karate, wouldn't you?" he asked her.

"You're going to owe me for this one, pal," she said, digging her forefinger into his ribs.

"I always pay off. You know that."

"Dearly, this time."

He kissed her on the cheek and left, wondering how the two women would get along.

He cabbed it to the Amalgamated Press and Wire Services Building on Dupont Circle and took the elevator up to David Hawk's office. He patted his pocket, making sure that he had his "cigars" with him.

"This is unexpected," Hawk said as Nick entered his office. "Sit down, N3."

"A lot of things have been unexpected, sir," Nick said, seating himself.

"Oh? Such as?"

"Such as you hanging me out to dry."

"What does that mean, exactly?"

"I think you know."

Hawk leaned forward and said, "Suppose you enlighten me, N3."

"First I think I should complete part of my assignment," Nick said.

"By all means."

From his pocket, Nick took the five silver tubes. He selected the biggest of the five, leaned forward, and put it on Hawk's desk.

"What's this?"

"I'm delivering the 'round peg' to the 'round hole,' sir," Nick explained. "Wasn't that what I was supposed to do?"

Hawk studied Nick for a few moments, then leaned forward wordlessly and picked up the silver tube.

"Yes, indeed, N3, that's what you were supposed to do."

THIRTY-NINE

"That was not, however, the sum total of your assignment," Hawk said.

"That was all I was told about, though," Nick pointed out. "The rest I was supposed to figure out for myself, right?"

"Correct."

"And I did. I was supposed to kill the person who has been killing our couriers."

"Which you did, in Switzerland."

"I killed one of them," Nick said, and Hawk raised his eyebrows.

"Are you suggesting that there were two killers?"

"No, sir," Nick said. "I'm not stopping at just two."

"Then how many?"

"Who knows?"

"Somebody does."

"Right."

Hawk rubbed his eyes with the thumb and forefinger of his right hand and said, "N3, you are beginning to make my head spin. If you have something to say, then say it."

"Let me get one thing straight in my mind first, sir."

"And what's that?"

"Was there ever a Dr. Lector?"

"Of course."

"And he's been under wraps all this time?"

"Under wraps," Hawk said, mulling the phrase over, and then said, "Yes."

"Here in Washington?"

"In a safe place."

"And there actually is a 'round peg' that has to be delivered to him?"

"It's already been delivered, thanks to you."

"Ah," Nick said. "I was the decoy. While the killer—or killers—were chasing me all over Europe, the real courier was delivering the 'round peg.' "

"Correct."

"Well, then, that part of the assignment was accomplished."

"Yes. There was a vital piece of information that Dr. Lector needed to continue his research, and he now has it."

"Whoopee . . ."

"I sense sarcasm in your tone, N3," Hawk said, not without a bit of the same.

"Maybe that's because I don't like being used as a decoy without being told . . . sir."

"Are you suggesting that I clear my decisions with you before I make them, N3?"

"Not at all, sir."

"In that case, I decided that you would make a more effective decoy if you were not aware that you were a decoy. That, I believe, was my right as your superior."

"Yes, sir."

"Do you have something else you want to discuss?"

"Just some drawings and a couple of dead people," Nick said.

"Drawings?"

"Yes, my roadmap," Nick said. He took all of the drawings out of his pocket and tossed them on the desk. "You'll see that as I went along, the drawings became more and more flagrant." He smoothed one out and said, "Here's one where the Colosseum figures prominently, which led me to

Rome. And here's the last one,'' he said, smoothing another out, ''where you can clearly make out the Washington Monument.''

Hawk leaned forward and threw a glance at the drawings, saying, ''Yes, I see.''

''You had somebody ahead of me all along, leaving these drawings for me to follow—and it must have been someone good.''

''You are not the only competent agent in this agency, N3,'' Hawk reminded Nick.

''I know that,'' Nick said. ''Yes, sir, I know that very well, but let's talk a little about two dead people in Switzerland.''

Hawk pursed his lips and built a little steeple from his fingertips, and that steeple seemed to be commanding all of his attention at the moment.

Nick Carter stood up; he was becoming too agitated to remain seated. He couldn't remember the last time he felt this way about the old man. He usually went along with everything and anything tossed his way by David Hawk, but the death of a couple of innocent people—well, he was having a little problem keeping that down.

''People die in our business, Nick,'' Hawk said. ''That's not something I should have to explain to you.''

''No, it isn't, sir. You're right about that, but these were two innocent people—unless there is still something I don't know,'' Nick added.

''You are correct again, N3,'' Hawk said, dropping his hands to the desk top and looking at Nick now. ''All of the people you met—the father and daughter in London, and the two people in Switzerland, who you didn't get a chance to meet—were all agents.''

''So they knew what was going on, too,'' Nick said. ''I was the only one in the dark, right?''

''No one knew all of what was going on,'' Hawk said, ''except for me. Everyone had his or her job to do.''

"Which was to keep me running around in circles, stalked by a killer, until he caught me and I killed him."

"Yes."

"And what if he had killed me?"

"Then I would have been very wrong about you, Nick."

"So what happened in Rome?"

"You will have to explain that."

Nick told Hawk about going to the apartment of Antonio Bellomo and finding the drawing, but no Bellomo, and then being shot at when he got downstairs.

"They knew I was going to be there."

"You might have been followed."

"Or your man might have been followed when he went to place the drawings."

"That would take more than one person," Hawk observed.

"Which means I'm right. There might be *a* killer, but whoever it is, has help."

"Like the man in Switzerland. It seems—" Nick started, then stopped and stood there, frowning.

"Finish your thought, N3."

"It just seems to me that nobody tried quite hard enough to kill me."

"I see," Hawk said. "You are dissatisfied with the opposition's actions."

"In that respect, I am," Nick said. "I think maybe they believed in my assignment as much as I did."

"Which means?"

"Which means that they not only wanted what I was carrying, they wanted Anton Lector, too. So everybody has been stringing each other along, except for me."

"You had to look like you really believed in what you were doing, N3. I thought that would be the best way to play it."

"All right," Nick said, and then he decided to sit down.

"What about Stephanie Clark? What's her role in all of this?"

"An unscheduled player."

"Yes, but she knew things she shouldn't have known," Nick said.

"For instance?"

It was then that Nick told Hawk that his "safe" line was no longer safe.

"That *is* disconcerting," Hawk admitted. "Why didn't you mention that to me when you contacted me?"

"I thought she might be working for you," Nick said without hesitation. "I didn't want to tip off either one of you that I suspected anything."

"It might have been easier if you had, but there's no point in going over what is already done." He opened his center drawer and took out a large brown envelope.

"I had a man go to Howard Clark's home and he came back with this." Hawk held up a photo. "It's a photograph of his daughter, Stephanie." Handing it to Nick, he said, "Is this the girl?"

Nick took the five-by-seven photo and examined it. It showed a lovely blonde girl in a bikini that showed off her excellent figure. The face was not entirely clear, but it looked like the girl he knew as Stephanie Clark.

"You couldn't come up with a better picture?"

"There were others when she was much younger, but this one appeared to be the most recent."

"Did you check further with the DIA?"

"Yes. They insist that no one has been using their machines without authority, but our computer people tell me that a knowledgeable person can do a lot of damage by simply using a telephone."

"He'd have to know certain codes, though, wouldn't he?"

"They would have to be armed with certain knowledge, yes," Hawk admitted.

"What about their machine having my name?"

"Again, denied by the DIA, but our people tell me that the DIA computer could very well have computed your next move, predicting where you would go next."

"You mean I've been matching wits with a computer?" Nick asked.

"It seems likely."

The idea of matching wits with a machine did not bother Nick so much as the possibility that he had been coming off second best in the contest.

Nick held the photograph up again and examined it as closely as he could. The girl in the picture was smiling; she had long blonde hair and well-rounded breasts that were barely covered by a skimpy bikini top. The bottom of the bathing suit was also brief, revealing quite a bit of anatomy that would not otherwise be seen outside of an intimate situation.

Which Nick, of course, had experienced with Stephanie Clark.

"I can't get a close enough look here," Nick said. "I'd like to go down to the lab and have them blow this up for me."

"By all means, if it will answer the question once and for all," Hawk said. "Let me know the results as soon as you get them."

"Yes, sir," Nick said, getting up. "Shouldn't take too long."

He left his superior's office and took the elevator down to the lab, where he handed the photo over to a technician. He asked for two blowups, one of the girl's upper torso, and one of her lower.

"This won't be difficult to take at all," the technician said, smiling. He told Nick to wait outside while he took the photo into the darkroom.

Nick sat down and examined his feelings about being used as an unwitting decoy. Facing it realistically, he had no beef.

He was one of the pawns and Hawk was the man who made the moves. That was the way this game went. As far as the dead people in Switzerland were concerned, as long as they were players, too, Nick could live with their deaths.

Whoever the courier killer was, he or she had had at least one helper—the man he had killed in the barn outside of Geneva. There had to be more than that, though. When the assignment started, he had been told that there was "someone" killing American couriers, but now it seemed possible—and even likely—that there was a "team" of killers. Still, every team had a coach, and that was the person Nick now had to concern himself with.

The technician came out with two damp blowups of the five-by-seven and handed them over.

"I hope you don't mind, but I made myself about a dozen copies," the man said.

"Thanks," Nick said, accepting the blowups and reclaiming the original.

One photo showed the face and upper body, which were now easily identifiable as those of Stephanie Clark.

Unless you looked very close.

The eyes, Nick noticed, were not quite the same, although he couldn't pinpoint what the difference was.

The other blowup was of the lower portion of the girl's body, cut off at the knees, though. Still, for someone who had been to bed with the girl, this part of her body was more easily recognizable.

Nick put the blowups down and put the five-by-seven into his pocket. He said to the technician, "Call David Hawk and tell him I'm on my way to Sandry Triggs' apartment. I want a team to meet me there as soon as possible. Got it?"

"I've got it—" the man said, but he had no time to say anything further, because Nick was already gone.

The decoy part of the assignment was over. It was time to end the other part, as well.

FORTY

Nick took an AXE car and drove to Sandry Triggs' apartment as quickly as possible. He had unwittingly—and probably needlessly—placed Sandry's life in jeopardy, and he hoped he could get there in time to undo it.

He parked illegally in front of the apartment house and rushed in. He waited impatiently for the elevator, and when it came, he catapulted into it and punched the button for Sandry's floor. When he got to her floor, he hadn't gone half the distance from the elevator to the apartment before he realized that the apartment door was open.

He took out his gun and entered the apartment warily, but he knew in his gut that the place was empty.

"Shit," he said quietly.

The apartment was not in a state of disarray, so it did not appear that there had been any kind of a struggle.

He walked through the apartment just as a matter of form, but it was empty, and there was still no indication that anyone had been taken out in a struggle.

He heard footsteps running down the hall and turned in time to greet an AXE team as they came through the door. Out of three men, he recognized one, a youngster named Ellis.

"Slow down, Ellis," he said. "We're too late."

"For what?" the kid asked.

"Nobody home."

"Should there have been?"

Nick nodded and Ellis turned to the other two men and said, "Look around."

"Do you know Sandry?" Nick asked.

"I've seen her," Ellis replied. "Cute little thing, right?"

"That's right," Nick said.

"This is her place, huh?"

Nick nodded, holding his gun at his side and glancing around the room in annoyance. Just out of a habit that he had acquired recently, he walked over to a small writing desk and rummaged through the trash can, but there was nothing there but trash.

"Sir?" one of the other men said from behind him. He turned to the man and saw that he was holding a piece of paper in his hand.

"Found this taped to the bathroom mirror," he said. He held it out in front of him for either Ellis or Nick to take, but Ellis kept his hands at his side and let the older, more experienced man have it.

It was brief and to the point: "Have both women, will be in touch. Have the item available."

"What item?" Ellis asked after he had also read it.

"A 'round peg,' " Nick said.

"Excuse me?"

Nick turned to the other two men and said, "Either one of you make a decent pot of coffee?"

They both looked at each other and Nick said, "Between the two of you, you should be able to figure it out."

"What are we going to do now?" Ellis asked as Nick holstered his gun.

"Wait," Nick said. "We're going to wait for a phone call with instructions."

"If this is a kidnapping, shouldn't we call in the FBI?" Ellis asked.

"This is not just a kidnapping, Ellis," Nick said. "We'll handle it ourselves."

"Yes, sir," Ellis said, responding to the authority in Nick's voice. "I'll check on the coffee."

Three agents in the kitchen making coffee, Nick thought bitterly, and Sandry was missing—or worse—thanks to him.

He picked up the phone and dialed a number that put him in touch with a room in the Amalgamated building.

He read off Sandry's phone number to the man who answered the phone and asked, "Is this a clean number?"

"Hold on."

All AXE employees' phones were checked frequently for bugging devices, and then filed as clean numbers until the next time they were checked.

The man came back on the line and said, "That is a clean line."

"Put me through to Hawk, will you, then?" Nick asked. He waited, listening to the clicks on the phone, and then Hawk was on the other end.

"They're gone, sir," he said, and explained about the note that had been left behind.

"I suppose you'll just have to sit there and wait for the call," Hawk said.

"That's what I figure on doing, sir."

"Since my number is no longer private," Hawk continued, "I will stay here until one of us receives a call."

"Good idea, sir."

"Thank you, N3," Hawk said. "I do get one once in a while."

"Yes, sir," Nick said, and Hawk hung up.

Nick hung up on his end and then decided to go to the kitchen to see what was holding up the coffee.

When the phone rang three hours later, Nick pounced on it.

"They called me just a minute ago, N3," Hawk's voice said. "Here are your instructions."

He gave them to Nick, and he knew that his superior was reciting from memory and had not written any of it down.

"They said that they will kill both women unless you come alone," Hawk finished. "The caller was a man."

"Then that's what I'll have to do, sir."

"Don't do anything foolish, N3," Hawk warned. "You have a team right there with you. Tell them what the instructions are and have them follow at a safe distance."

"Yes, sir," Nick lied. "I will."

"I have to go out," Nick told Ellis and the other two men after he hung up. "Wait here in case they call."

Ellis nodded, and they turned to a deck of cards.

FORTY-ONE

Nick's instructions were to come alone to an abandoned building that was near the old federal building, and to bring the "item" with him. He parked his AXE car two blocks from the location and proceeded from there on foot. Of course he didn't have the "round peg" with him. All he had were four cigars in silver tubes to use as bait.

The building in question took up the entire block, with exits and entrances on all sides. The building was forever changing hands, but so far no one had ever done anything with it, and it remained empty.

Nick had instructions to enter from the front, but he figured he could always claim confusion, since the place had so many different entrances.

He chose a fire escape on the side nearest him. Jumping as high as he could, he caught hold of the bottom rung of the ladder and tried to control the speed with which it came down. As cavernous as the building was, the slightest noise might echo through, announcing his arrival.

He climbed up the ladder, then slid it up after him, just in case anyone checked. He turned then and climbed two flights of steps until he reached a window on the third floor. He was not as prepared for breaking and entering as he would have liked, but he found the window unlocked and was able to enter in relative silence.

He found himself in a small office on a floor that was separated into many small offices. He had no idea where in the building they were holding Sandry and Stephanie, but he did know what entrance he was expected to use to make his delivery, and he would have to go from there.

Moving out into the hall, the first decision he made was to avoid elevators. They were noisy and would announce his presence in the building. Whether he went up or down, he was going to use stairways.

Ideally, he would have liked locating the women before he took any action, but given the size of the building, that did not appear to be likely. What he intended to do was make his way through the building to the entrance he was expected to use, and then see who was waiting for him.

There were no lights on in the hall and, for all Nick knew, no electricity anywhere in the building. Having rushed there from Sandry's apartment, he was unprepared for that condition. He stood stock still in the hallway, listening intently while he waited for his eyes to adjust themselves to the gloom. Once he was able to see somewhat, he began to move down the hall, picking a direction at random. His gun remained in its holster because it was not a shoot-first situation. Before there was any shooting, he had to find Sandry.

He moved along the hallway, passing both closed and opened doorways. The open rooms were obviously empty; the closed doors had no light showing beneath them, and that was good enough for him. Finally, he came to the end of the hall and a doorway which led to a stairwell.

Tempted to go up, where he felt the women might be, he nevertheless started down, a mental picture in his mind of where he had come in, and where they were expecting him to come in.

When he came to a landing that should have been the second floor, he found that there was no second floor. Instead, the door opened out onto a catwalk, high above the first floor below. Stepping gingerly out onto the walk, he peered down and searched for any kind of light, even a candle, but there was nothing. If they were down there, they were waiting for him in the dark. His mental map said that if he walked straight out on this catwalk, he would eventually be above the point where he had been instructed to enter. Of course, there was always the chance that a man had been stationed on this very catwalk, or the one to his right that ran parallel with his.

With this in mind, he drew his gun and started walking forward as carefully as possible. He did not want to set off even the tiniest vibration on the walk, lest it be felt by someone waiting at the other end. He kept one eye ahead of him and one eye cast down, which was a feat accomplished by years of practice.

Suddenly, he caught a small flash of light and stopped. It was down on the floor, and he stood stock still and waited for it to appear again. When it did, he realized that it was a flashlight with someone's hand clasped over it to shield the light. Whoever was holding it had carelessly opened his fingers too wide on two occasions, and Nick had caught sight of it both times.

At least one, then, on the floor level.

Moving forward again, he kept both eyes ahead of him, attempting to verify a theory he had just formed. As a reward, he caught a flash of light ahead, just a small sliver, and when he looked down, he caught a return flash. They were staying in contact with each other via flashlight, and in doing so had given away their positions.

He had them.

All he had to worry about now was the existence of a third party—or even more. He stood still and tried to decide where he would have placed a third man. He watched closely, waiting for other slivers of light, but when there were none, he had to assume that his reception committee was two.

He began moving again, even slower. He did not want to walk into one of his welcoming committee. That wouldn't do at all. He was going to either grab the man on the catwalk and have him take him to where the women were, or else dispose of the man above and grab the man below for the same purpose.

He'd have to play it by ear and see how conditions presented themselves.

Nick was moving one foot next to the other, instead of one foot in front of the other, and suddenly he saw the man, crouched over and peering down at the floor. He could have put his foot against the man's backside and catapulted him into the air, but that would have alerted the one on the lower level. Instead, he put his gun away and took Hugo out. Holding the knife ahead of him, he continued to shuffle toward the unwary man until he was able to put the point of the knife behind the man's left ear. The man stiffened and Nick increased the pressure until the tip of the knife drew a drop of blood.

"Stand up," he whispered, and the man obeyed immediately. Nick patted him down and came up with an automatic, which he tucked into his belt.

"Is there a way down up ahead?" he asked.

The man nodded and said, "Y-yeah. There's a stairway that leads right downstairs."

"Let's go."

He left the man's flashlight lying on the floor of the catwalk and marched him ahead.

"If you stay quiet, you stay alive," he told the man, who nodded anxiously.

When they reached the stairway, Nick kept the man one step ahead of him. He had his left hand on his left shoulder and the knife tucked securely behind his ear.

When they reached the bottom, Nick pulled back on the man's shoulder to stop him. He leaned forward and spoke directly into the man's ear.

"Now we walk to your friend. Tell him you're coming when I tap you on the shoulder."

The man nodded and Nick gave him a push to get him started. As they approached the other man, Nick waited until he could make out the shape of him, then tapped his man on the shoulder.

"Eddie, it's me," he said, almost too loud.

"Jesus!" the other man exclaimed. "You scared the shit out of me." He shone the flashlight toward Nick and the other man and started to say, "What the hell—" as Nick took the automatic from his belt, raised it over his man's head, and clubbed him. At the same time, the other man saw the move and shouted, "Hey!"

The second man moved faster than Nick had anticipated. As the first man slumped down, the second came barreling into both of them. The combined weight of the two men knocked Nick back, and when he hit the ground, the automatic was jarred loose from his hand.

The second man was using his flashlight to try and locate Nick, and although the light hurt his eyes, Nick could see the shape of the gun in the man's other hand. The last thing he wanted was a shot to be fired.

Still grasping Hugo in his right hand, he rolled to his left just as the flashlight was about to spot him. Gathering his legs underneath him, he sprang at the man, grabbing for the hand that held the gun. They both went tumbling to the floor, and as they rolled about, the man started to club Nick with the flashlight. Before he could do more damage, Nick drove Hugo straight into the man's belly. Air escaped through the man's mouth as if he were a punctured balloon. Nick felt him go limp, but twisted the knife just to make sure he wasn't playing possum.

Convinced that the man was dead, he pulled Hugo free, stood up, and kicked the dead man's gun away into the darkness. He turned and repeated the action with the first man's automatic. After that, he picked up the flashlight, took out the batteries, and scattered them into the darkness as well. That done, he turned his attention to the first man, who was coming to on the floor, moaning and holding his head.

"Come here," he ordered the man, grabbing him by the collar and pulling him over to the dead man. "That's your friend, and this is the knife that killed him," Nick said, pushing the bloodied knife underneath the man's nose. "Smell his blood? Want to taste it?"

The man surprised Nick by turning over and vomiting onto the cement floor. Nick waited for the man's retching to subside, then pulled him away from the foul-smelling puddle and the dead body.

"What are you, hired muscle?" Nick asked.

"Ahh," the man said, clearing his throat, and then rasped, "Yeah."

"Where are the two women?"

The man answered without hesitating.

"Go up the other catwalk. There's a stairway over there," he said, pointing into the darkness. "Walk to the end and go up the steps. They're in one of the offices up there."

That was the same floor Nick had come in on, but on the other side of the building.

"What's your interest beyond money?" Nick asked.

"None, I swear."

"You want to buy in or take a walk?"

"I'll walk, Mister. Believe me, I'll walk."

"Okay," Nick said, pulling the man to his feet. "Walk."

As the man turned to leave, Nick pulled Wilhelmina out and slugged the man behind his other ear. Nobody could say he didn't have a heart.

He walked through the darkness to the stairway, climbed up to the catwalk, and hurried along it to the other end. When he came to the stairwell, he ran up to the third floor, then stopped when he came to the closed stairwell door. He opened it slowly and peered down the hall. There was a dim light coming from one of the open doorways, and it flickered as if it were candlelight. He eased his way down the hall toward the door and suddenly heard a woman's voice say, "I told those assholes to get some storm lamps, and they bring candles." The tone of her voice was thick with disgust.

It was plainly the voice of the woman he knew as Stephanie Clark.

He stepped into the room with his gun in plain sight, and both Sandry Triggs and "Stephanie Clark" turned to look at him.

Sandry was bound and gagged, but her eyes were trying frantically to send him a message.

Stephanie stared at him, looking shocked, and then suddenly smiled as if she were very pleased to see him.

"Nick! Thank God you're here!"

She had been seated on the floor and now she stood up and said, "I just managed to work myself loose and was about to untie Sandry. How did you get past those men?"

"What's your real name?" he asked her.

She frowned and said, "What do you mean?"

Nick took the five-by-seven photo from his pocket and held it so she could look at it.

"This is a picture of Stephanie Clark," he said. "You can't see it very well from there, but trust me when I say that she's got a birthmark just below her navel—a birthmark that you don't have." He threw the picture aside and it fluttered to the floor. "So who are you, and where's the real Stephanie Clark?"

"You're crazy," she said.

"Come off it," he said. "I heard you just before I came in. And if I needed further proof, there's the fact that you're both up here with no guard. Sandry's tied up and you're not."

"I told you," she insisted, "I just worked my way free."

"Really?" Nick said. "And what did you do with the rope, eat it?"

He indicated the floor around her, where there was no rope or binding of any kind that she might have just worked free of.

"It's over, lady. Your days as a courier killer are no more and all because you got greedy."

"What do you mean?"

"You not only wanted what I was carrying, but the man I was to deliver it to; otherwise you could have killed me any one of several times. And the times you did fire at me, or have some hired gun fire at me, were just to convince me that the killer was on my trail and to keep me moving toward my goal."

"Did you bring the item with you?" she asked, as if oblivious to the fact that he was holding a gun on her.

"You mean the item I carried with me all over Europe?" he asked. "Sure, I brought it." He reached into his pocket for the four silver tubes and said, "Here it is."

She stared at him, then said, "Your cigars! You never smoked them. Of course!"

"Of course," he repeated. "Here, catch."

He tossed them to her, one at a time, and she caught them and held them in her hands.

"Which one?" she demanded.

"All of them," he said. "None of them. Any of them. Take your pick, they all contain the same thing."

She broke the seal of one, opened it, and took out a cigar. She shredded it and let the pieces fall to the floor. She then repeated the ritual with each of the other three.

"Cigars," she said. "They're just cigars."

"That's right."

She stared at him in disbelief, and then she said, "A decoy? They used Nick Carter as a decoy?"

He grinned and said, "That's almost as unbelievable as using me as a courier, isn't it?"

She just stood there shaking her head, and he said, "Quite a world, huh? Can't trust anybody to run true to form. Okay, lady, what did you do with the real Stephanie Clark?"

"She's long dead," the woman replied. "I took her place months ago. I'm almost an exact double, you know, what with a nip here and a tuck there."

"Except for her birthmark. Pretty careless for a smart girl like you, huh?"

She made an ugly face and then started to move toward Sandry.

"Oh, no," Nick said. "Stay put, lady."

"I'll untie her for you," she said. "It's all over, isn't it? She's been trussed up like that for hours. Maybe she's suffocating."

She kept moving toward the other girl, and Nick said, "Lady, don't."

"Who would have believed that they'd use you as a courier, and then a decoy?" she asked. "Maybe a few other things I heard about you were wrong, too."

"Like what?"

"Like maybe you wouldn't shoot a woman."

Nick shook his head sadly and said, "Don't bet on it."

The woman took one more step, then stopped and stared at Nick.

"No," she said. "No, I don't think I will. You're probably one hell of a card player, Nick. Aren't you?"

"Only when the chips are down," he said, and then moved to untie Sandry himself.

EPILOGUE

"Her name is Natalie Fortune, née Fortunelli," Hawk said. "She's a computer expert. She must have taken Stephanie Clark's place four months ago, as she said, and then started using the DIA computer to locate couriers."

"Then she'd use hired help," Nick continued. "Hoods, mercenaries, anyone she could find to work for a price and do her dirty work for her."

Hawk closed her file and dropped it on his desk top.

"I wonder if Howard Clark had any contact with her during the past four months?" Hawk said distractedly.

"He was too good a man not to recognize the fact that she wasn't his daughter."

"Killing him killed the proverbial two birds with one stone, I suppose," Hawk mused.

Nick nodded, then picked up her file and began to leaf through it absently.

"I suppose you're pretty lucky, N3," Hawk said.

"How's that, sir?"

"If she hadn't been greedy, as you said, you might be another victim now, instead of sitting here waiting for another assignment."

Nick closed the folder and dropped it back on his boss' desk.

"Another assignment, already?" he asked. "Like the last

one? Going to hang me out to dry again? Dangle me like a worm on a hook? Throw me to the—''

''Please, spare us the benefit of your vast knowledge of clichés, N3,'' Hawk said with a pained look.

''I'll tell you what,'' Nick said, standing up. ''How about you going out on the next one, and I'll sit behind the desk for a while.''

Hawk's eyebrows went up as he considered the remark, and then he said, ''You know, N3, that might prove quite interesting.''

Nick stared at David Hawk, then shook his head and said, ''You're giving in too easily.'' He sat down. ''All right, what's the next one?''

He swore that he saw a fleeting look, a smugness, pass over Hawk's face as the old man opened a drawer and took out a large, brown envelope.

Outfoxed by the old fox again.

DON'T MISS THE NEXT NEW NICK CARTER SPY THRILLER

EARTHFIRE NORTH

Lydia Coatsworth's mouth started to go dry again and she began to have second thoughts about what she was doing. She didn't need this, she told herself. She was a scientist, not a private eye.

Still, there was the door and behind it . . . what? Proof?

Summoning up her courage, she tried the door. It was unlocked. Inside, it was pitch dark. She groped along the wall for a light switch, found it, and a caged bulb flashed on overhead.

She stood in a large, immaculately clean, tiled room. On the wall in front of her was a series of dials and valves set into a burnished metal control panel. The constant humming told her that a gigantic engine of some sort was at work somewhere beneath her.

In the next room, a piece of machinery the size of a small house stood in one corner on a bed of massive timbers. She threw back a piece of the protective covering. The machine looked familiar somehow. The tag dangling from a valve wheel was in German. It gave the port of origin as Mainz. Mainz . . . what did she know about Mainz? Then it struck her. Mainz was where Stauben and Sons had their foundry.

They were the largest manufacturers of nuclear reactor components in the world!

She threw back more of the cover. It was coming back to her now. All of it. This was a type of water pump that regulated the amount of coolant to a reactor's core. A nuclear reactor. What on earth would anyone want with a nuclear reactor in Iceland?

Tires crunched on the cinders outside, the sound coming through a ventilation pipe. A car door slammed.

Quickly she tried to cover the pump, but she could not get the plastic sheet over the top. She gave up, and started for the door.

In the pump room, she dashed down the stairs to the main floor. Maybe here among the pipes she would be able to conceal herself until it was safe to leave. She hadn't done anything illegal, yet she had a very odd feeling about this place . . . for starters, who would run off leaving the door to a nuclear reactor building site open?

The door at the top of the stairs flew open with a bang, and the lights went on. To her horror, she saw a line of footprints in the dust leading from the bottom of the stairs to where she hid. Christ! She bit her tongue to keep from crying out.

He came down the stairs like a hunter stalking his prey, stopping every few feet to cock his head as if he was listening for something. It was the man in the mechanic's overalls. She caught a glimpse of him through the tangle of pipes. A huge black revolver rode in his right hand.

He'd found the footprints and was looking in her direction now. Instinctively she cowered lower into her tiny refuge, and felt her foot wedge between two pipes.

He came slowly toward where she was hiding, and their eyes met. He brought the pistol up, and came the rest of the way . . .